CAPTAIN HAZZARD *in...*

the *Python Men*
of the
Lost City

by **RON FORTIER** *and* **CHESTER HAWKS**

with Illustrations by **ROB DAVIS**

AIRSHIP 27 PRODUCTIONS

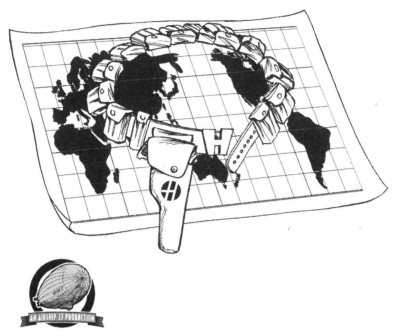

CAPTAIN HAZZARD : THE PYTHON MEN OF LOST CITY
by Ron Fortier and Chester Hawks
Copyright © 2009

An Airship 27 Production
www.airship27.com
www.airship27hangar.com

Associate Editor: John Bruening
Cover © 2009 Mark Maddox
Interior illustrations and design © 2009 Rob Davis

ISBN-13: 978-0615696492
ISBN-10:061569649X

Third Edition- First Airship 27 Productions, Publisher edition
Printed in the United States of America

10 9 8 7 6 5 4 3 2 1

Contents

THE ONE-SHOT WONDER

By Norman Hamilton

For many years, pulp enthusiasts loved to talk about the one-shot hero, Captain Hazzard. Hazzard had appeared in one issue of his own title, dated May 1938, from publisher A.A. Wyn's Magazine Publishers Inc. The dramatic, beautiful cover by Norm Saunders, portrayed a handsome, bronzed, chiseled-faced hero attempting to save a beautiful blond damsel in the distress from the clutches of *The Python Men of the Lost City*. It was pretty heady stuff, and clearly intended as a Doc Savage rip-off. The following month the title was gone and Captain Hazzard drifted into pulp obscurity. Or so he should have. But pulp fans are persistent if nothing else, and loyal to their heroes, even those heroes who only make one appearance.

Over the subsequent years, long after A.A. Wyn's outfit had morphed into the paperback company known as Ace Books, lovers of pulps kept Hazzard's memory alive by reprinting his one and only story over and over again. All legal rights to the character and story had long since expired and thus fallen into public domain. Somewhere in the late 1960s, comic fan Ron Fortier purchased a facsimile copy of the book from long time pulp historian and collector, Robert Weinberg. Fortier became intrigued by the character and promised himself to one day revive him if the circumstances were favorable.

Meanwhile, other pulp historians had been doing their own research into Captain Hazzard, and bit by bit a skeletal story about the hero and his origins began to emerge. In 1934, Wyn had hired a former Street & Smith editor, Paul Chadwick, to write for his line. Chadwick became the first, and principle, writer of their new Secret Agent X series. X was a bizarre attempt by Wyn's editors to combine the attributes of both the Shadow and Doc Savage into one hero. X was a master of disguises who operated as an independent agent battling America's foes. Chadwick's stories, and those of the writers who followed him, were published under the house name Brant House (obviously someone had a sense of humor). Chadwick wrote the bloodiest X stories and stayed with the character until 1936, when sales began to drop off.

Somewhere in all this, Chadwick had married a woman named Dorothy Lester. Dorothy had once been Lester Dent's personal secretary during the early days of his work on the legendary pulp hero, Doc Savage — a little known fact worth keeping in mind as our tale progresses. When Chadwick's editors came to him with the assignment to create and write a hero in the mold of the Man of Bronze, one has to believe he was savvy enough to pick his wife's brain for advice.

The similarities between Captain Hazzard and Doc Savage would be many. Both were super-intelligent and possessed many academic degrees. Giving a hero an honorific like *doctor* or *captain* was standard practice in the pulps. Both men would have a unique base of operations in or around New York City. Doc's was his suite/lab on the 86th Floor of the Empire State Building, while the Champion of Justice maintained an entire complex out on Long Island called Hazzard Labs. Each would go off on globe-trotting adventures accompanied by a group of highly loyal, brilliant and colorful aides. They each employed futuristic-like technology, arming themselves with all kinds of outlandish gizmos used in the fight against evildoers.

Here's how Chadwick verbally painted his new pulp star: "His name was Captain Hazzard. He was young, ruggedly built, broad-shouldered, dark-haired, with a face that was a mixture of dynamic youth and mature power. It was hard to place his age. He seemed to be in his middle twenties. He might have been younger or older. There was a changeable quality in his blue-gray eyes as there was about his face. The irises had the clearness of blue flame, and darker glints glowed beneath."

There were a few notable differences to set the two heroes apart, the primary one of these being Hazzard's gift of ESP (extra-sensory perception). In the prologue, we are told that at an early age, his parents were murdered and he was blinded. Attending a school for the blind, the lad began to rely on his other senses, which had become heightened – a common occurrence among many blind people. But what was unexpected is that young Hazzard began to demonstrate extraordinary telepathic skills. By the time he was a teen, he could "see" things with his mind and transmit those images to others who were likewise gifted. When an operation restored Hazzard's sight, he swore an oath to dedicate his life to fighting evil and injustice wherever they appeared in the world. To this end he would put his amazing mental and physical strengths.

Chadwick was comfortable writing suspense, urban melodramas posing as pseudo detective mysteries. But Captain Hazzard was high adventure. That Chadwick was out of his element is clearly evident in his putting African pythons in a South American setting (although Anaconda Men of the Lost City clearly wouldn't have had the same zip as the actual title).]

The story Chadwick turned in is full of plot holes and under-developed characters whose names change from one chapter to another, making it difficult to keep track of who's who. Most pulp tales were knocked off speedily. That was the hallmark of the style – write fast and often, or else don't get paid at the end of the week. Still, the poor quality of this particular book would indicate Chadwick's lack of enthusiasm for the project. One has to wonder if he really did not care if it succeeded or not.

Of course, it did not – not only because of the substandard quality, but by 1938 the country was in the midst of the Great Depression, and many companies were having to cut back on their output. By the time *Captain Hazzard: Python Men of the Lost City* was released, its fate was predetermined, and so it disappeared into literary history. It would go on to exist in reprint after reprint until 2006, when Fortier, the one-time fan now turned professional writer, took it upon himself to bring back the Champion of Justice in a brand new series of pulp novel adventures.

Fortier launched the new Captain Hazzard series by first going back into the original and fixing it. He filled in the plot holes, reshaped the characters, defined them more clearly and added entirely new chapters to drive the narrative. By the time he was finished, an old, nearly forgotten pulp hero was ready once again to take on the minions of evil. Fortier enhanced certain story elements that previously had been given cursory attention, like the white scar that runs across Hazzard's left eye, the one visible reminder of his sightless youth and the murder of his parents. Now, when Hazzard becomes impassioned, the tiny white line reddens noticeably – an indication he is about to go into action. Fortier also revealed the hero's full Christian name as Kevin Douglas Hazzard. With the success of this revamped classic, Fortier and his Airship 27 Productions have gone on to bring us three additional Captain Hazzard novels; *Citadel of Fear* (co-written with Martin Powell), *Curse of the Red Maggot* and last year's *Cavemen of New York*. Fortier plans to begin work on a fifth novel later this year. He hopes to continue writing them as long as pulp fans want to read them.

You hold in your hand the second edition of a fast-paced, action-packed pulp thriller penned by Paul Chadwick (writing as Chester Hawks) and Ron Fortier – two writers separated by time and space but brought together by a love for pulp fiction. And that is how a one-shot wonder became a seventy-year-old classic pulp survivor. Not a bad story.

CAPTAIN HAZZARD

in

PYTHON MEN OF THE LOST CITY

by

Chester Hawks & Ron Fortier

Introducing · Capt. Hazzard

When we finished writing the chronicle of the "Python Men of the Lost City," the editor asked us for a brief word of introduction for this column. To tell the truth, I didn't know where to begin. For in the story, we told of how Captain Hazzard had been blind for fifteen years of his boyhood; and how he had studied and developed his mental powers far beyond those of an average person; how he had regained his eyesight, and then marshalled a group of assistants – scientists, chemists, mathematicians, adventurers –

and raised a challenge to the criminals of the world. So we were at a loss as to how to give you a real insight into the character of this remarkable man – until Hawks remembered what had happened on that glorious day when Hazzard's eyesight was restored to him.

As the doctor unwound the bandages over the lad's eyes, he warned that the eyes could only be used for three minutes the first day. Young Kevin Douglas Hazzard reached out and took my arm, saying:

"There are things I want to see. Will you get them for me, Hawks?"

I squeezed his arm in reply. In a quiet voice, Hazzard made his first request:

"Let me see a picture of my mother and father."

That choked us all up. For both of his parents had died while he was blind. He had known and loved them, but had never seen their faces. "You shall see that picture," Hawks said.

His next request was a simple one. Most of you see it every day of your lives. Hazzard's voice had a strange thrill in it when he asked:

"I want to see the American flag. Those stars, and the red, white and blue must be a beautiful thing to see."

I assured him that a person has to look a long way to see a more beautiful thing than Old Glory. And then came the his last request:

"The picture of Blind Justice – the lady holding the scales, with the blindfold over her eyes. I want to be her eyes from this day forth."

Well, readers, this is the best way we knew of introducing a brave, dashing and sincere man – Captain Hazzard, champion of justice!

Chester Hawks

CHAPTER ONE

The Murder Curtain

Three men stood beside a dusty gray auto at one side of Pier 52, North River, and watched the American liner *Liberty* slide into berth. Their faces mirrored a tension mixed with a haunting, brooding dread. Some hidden conflict seemed to be twisting their nerves to spring-like tautness. Stark terror of a force outside themselves was lashing them pitilessly to do a thing they feared.

Dusk had come and gone hours earlier, leaving a sprinkling of stars amidst a cloudy night sky. Floodlights bathed the pier as the great ship touched the dock with a rumble of winches, a clatter of gangplanks, a shuffling of feet. White-coated stewards carrying luggage were the first to reach the pier. Then came the passengers, smiling, waving, calling excited greetings to friends and loved ones on hand to welcome them home.

But there was no love, no friendship in the eyes of the three men who stood beside the dusty, queer-looking auto.

One was tall, thin-lipped, with a sickly pallor accentuated by blue-black hair. Another had a powerful body, a heavy bloated face. The third was small, swarthy, vicious, his sharp teeth showing in a servile, hyena grin. He wore goggles and a chauffeur's cap.

They made no move to meet anybody. They stared fixedly through the door of the pier shed at the lights of the great liner. Not until all the passengers were off the ship and through customs did the tall, pallid man stoop and whisper something to the one with the bloated face. The heavy man nodded, set off at a fast walk diagonally across the street.

The swarthy chauffeur slipped behind the wheel of the gray car and started the motor. He sat on the front seat with the alertness of a cat waiting to spring. The pallid man climbed into the back and drew the side shades carefully. The car waited, its engine purring.

But something moved on the roof of the car as the man inside slowly cranked a handle. It might have been a collapsible radio aerial.

It rose up thinly, forming a tripod. The handle inside continued to move. From the top of the tripod, thick black rods pushed out of a tubular metal framework. They were slender, almost invisible to anyone standing more than a few feet away. But they crisscrossed into a design that was horribly like the antennae of some great insect.

There were still finer, hairlike rods branching out from them and these trembled with the vibration of the car's engine, reminiscent of the feelers of a giant deadly centipede getting ready to strike.

The man inside ceased turning the handle. He crouched forward, staring through a peephole in the side curtains at the big pier entrance. Once he moved to another peephole on the opposite side of the car and glanced intently in the direction that the bloated-faced man had gone.

There was an empty store diagonally across the street here, its windows broken and dusty. Dimly seen on the roof of this building was the rod framework of another small tripod. The hairlike antennae were invisible, but the metal tubes in which they were mounted reflected a faint gleam of light.

The dark-haired man's pallor increased, and his hands trembled. He again took up his station at the peephole nearest the dock. His black eyes held a savage gleam of impending murder.

There was excitement at the top of the *Liberty's* forward gangplank now. Several dapper ship's officers led a strange looking figure forward, a stowaway who had been discovered in one of the holds after the vessel had come through quarantine.

The stowaway's clothing was tattered, stained, his body emaciated. But the most startling thing about him was his face. It had the dry, scaly look of a reptile. All life seemed to have gone from the skin. Brown, dead looking, it cracked into unsymmetrical sections like the hide of an alligator.

Several officers kept at a distance from him, as though they feared that he might be contaminated. But two immigration officers, accustomed to handling all sorts of queer characters, came up and grabbed him by the arms. One said: "Come along, buddy. We're gonna take you places."

The reptile-faced man made no answer. His dull, glazed eyes were focused on some horror only he could see. He moved sluggishly, letting himself be pulled forward. The few people left on the dock recoiled as he passed, staring with wide-eyed amazement.

The immigration officers led him through the pier shed toward the exit. Here another man, short, stocky, keen-faced, pleasant looking, was lingering purposely. He stepped forward as the trio reached him. In his hands was a small notebook and pencil, freshly sharpened. On his jacket lapel was pinned a small card with the word PRESS printed on it. "My name's Crawley," he said. "Any idea where that chap came from? I picked up a message on the ship-to-shore telephone and heard about the stowaway."

One of the immigration officers waved him back. "You press people give me a pain," he muttered. "Our department will make a report when it's ready."

"The *Liberty* put in at several South American ports," persisted Crawley. "Maybe this man's an escaped prisoner from Devil's Island."

"Yes, and maybe he isn't!" snapped the officer.

Crawley shrugged, stepped aside. But he followed at a distance, feverishly jotting down notes from his keen-eyed observations. His own car was parked outside along the block. He had instructions to learn the identity of this strange man who had somehow stowed away on a crack passenger liner.

He was fifty feet behind when the stowaway and the two immigration men passed through the exit. For a moment they were on a line with the gray car parked outside the pier and the metal tripod mounted up there in the darkness on top of the empty store building. Crawley was the first immediate witness of the shocking, extraordinary thing that occurred.

The night gloom outside the pier entrance changed suddenly. It grew lighter, with a wavering, eerie incandescence, as though the sky had been fired with the glow of an aurora borealis. Tongues of shimmering, uncanny light slid through the air, wavered, intermingled, touched and retreated, only to reappear again. But they were not in the sky. They were in the air close to the earth, forming a weird, pulsating, radiant curtain between the tripod on the gray car and the one on the roof of the building. It was a curtain of horrible death, for the stowaway with the reptile-like face and the two immigration officers who stood paralyzed in this ghastly web of writhing fire.

Muscles strained under their clothing. Veins stood out on their faces, swelled, seemed about to burst like over-ripe grapes. Their eyes started from their heads. Their mouths opened, tongues protruding. Fearful, smothered cries ripped from their quivering throats.

The two immigration officers sagged on legs gone limp as jelly. The stowaway took two jerky steps forward. He seemed to possess an inhuman stamina, for he almost stumbled out of the curtain of light. Then he too paused, staggered and dropped.

William Crawley did a strange thing for a reporter – a strange thing in the face of that maelstrom of murder. He calmly closed his eyes, seemed to go to sleep. His features looked peaceful, trancelike for a moment. He seemed almost bored by the terror of the night. What went on in his mind made no show in the visible world. But odd systolic vibrations stirred in the inner, unknown realms of etheric space. Crawley's horror and the image that fell on the retina of his eyes was transferred in the flash of a split second by telepathic influence to the brain of another man ten miles away.

This man was working diligently in a private chamber of a great complex on Long Island. The compound was made up of a half dozen structures, including several sophisticated laboratories, a mechanical workshop and two huge airplane hangars. There were high walls of reinforced concrete around the entire estate, electrically charged barbed wire on top of that, and then other walls of steel and hardwood. Still Crawley's mental image, his feelings, made their way through these barricades by telepathic impulse with the speed of light.

At the first twinge of the reporter's psychic signal, this unique man put down the equipment he had been calibrating and touched the fingers of his right hand to his temple. Closing his eyes, he breathed deeply and thought the single word: SEND.

Immediately this fellow began receiving the same images, the same impressions of horror. His mind, connected by the mysterious bond of extra-sensory impressions – which make up the new science of telepathy and clairvoyance, known collectively as parapsychology - actually seemed to see through the eyes of the newshound on the scene. The impressions came dimly at first, wavering, disturbing, out of a fog apparently, like an image from a projector being focused. Then they were clear, true, awful as the thing itself. And the man in the laboratory continued breathing deeply, gripping the edge of his table with tense fingers, staring fixedly at the blank wall before him.

His name was Kevin Douglas Hazzard. He was young, ruggedly built, broad-shouldered, dark haired, with a face that was a mixture of dynamic youth and mature power. A neatly trimmed mustache reminded many of the actor Clark Gable. It was hard to place Hazzard's age. He seemed to be in his middle twenties. He might have been younger or older. There was a changeable quality in his blue-gray eyes as there was about his face. The irises had the clearness of a blue flame, but when his moods varied, a wind seemed to blow across the flame, and darker glints glowed beneath.

He was a man about whom many legends had sprung up. Many strange stories had been told of his actions, his powers, his career. But hardly any of them as startling as the truth itself.*

*"His mind, connected by the mysterious bond of extra-sensory impressions...
actually seemed to see through the eyes of the newshound on the scene."*

AUTHOR'S NOTES *

Captain Hazzard, America's Ace Adventurer, was blinded in infancy and spent the first fifteen years of his life in total darkness. Denied normal pleasures and activities, he had been thrown back on himself, on his own cleverness and imagination. He had learned the Braille system of reading by sense of touch. More than this, in those long dark years when the outer world was beyond his sight, he had developed his latent mental powers to the point where they extended much farther than that of the average person. He had studied all the phenomena of the mind: hypnotism, the various schools of psychology, Yoga and other forms of Oriental mysticism including the shamanistic beliefs and practices of the Lamas of Tibet, and telepathy.

When a delicate surgical operation had finally restored his physical sight, he had dedicated his life to adventure, action, and the extension of man's knowledge of the world about him. He had gathered together certain chosen assistants, brilliant young scientists, chemists, mathematicians, adventurers. A few hand-picked men he tested for telepathic powers by means of card symbols, using the method of Doctor Rhine of Duke University. In this way, he had formed a small group of close associates who could send mental messages and images to him, and receive his in turn under certain conditions. The telepathic powers of the mind are not yet perfect, but someday, when the world is older, Captain Hazzard believes they will be. The common experiences which people everywhere have of telepathy, mind-reading, foresight, and psychic contact prove that mankind is on the threshold of new and more vast discoveries in the realm of the mind. Captain Hazzard is a pioneer in this great new branch of science.

And his brilliant research and inventions in his Long Island laboratory, as well as his startling world adventures, have brought him not only wealth and fame, but recognition from his government. For certain secret advice of a military nature, which has helped to make America safe against foreign attack, he has been given the honorary rank of captain in both the army and navy air corps.

In his mind's eye, Hazzard saw the stowaway pitch forward. He saw the two immigration men lying in huddled heaps. He saw for an instant, as did Crawley, that one end of that weird curtain of death was somehow connected with the parked gray car.

He stood at ease while the action unfolded, while Crawley, his agent, continued to send out the telepathic impulses that were registering in his own excited brain.

The strange curtain of livid light disappeared as suddenly as it had appeared. It flashed off, leaving the darkness darker. And in that darkness, the grinning chauffeur behind the wheel of the gray car touched levers and the car sped away.

Crawley pointed, cried through trembling lips: "Those men did it!" A policeman heard him, ran for a patrol car. Crawley himself turned and raced for the spot down the street where his own coupe was parked. He swung it around, tore after the gray car that was now only a ghostly blur up the long waterfront street.

Keeping the gray car's headlamps in sight, Crawley pushed his smaller auto faster, taking one sharp turn after another, not wanting to lose what he believed to be the story of a lifetime.

Captain Hazzard, in his private sanctum, grabbed the table's edge still more tightly, as though he himself were driving Crawley's coupe. Slowly it gained on the gray car. A police radio cruiser with a powerful motor nosed up and passed Crawley. It continued to outpace him, creeping up on the gray car ahead. Crawley stepped on the gas, hugged the wheel more tightly.

Then Captain Hazzard gasped and turned from his work bench as an idea struck him. He broke into the telepathic reception he was getting from Crawley, sent out a mental warning of his own: "Look back, Crawley! There may be another car behind you. Tripod! Curtain of death!"

The message flashed through etheric space to Crawley's mind. Crawley got it, faintly at first, then more clearly as he felt the powerful brain impulse of Captain Hazzard. He looked up at his rearview mirror and hastily adjusted it. Then his mouth opened in surprise. Coming up behind him was a second gray sedan with a duplicate tripod affixed to its roof.

Crawley jerked his steering wheel to the right and bounced over the curb just as a flash of hot light sizzled through the air, ripping up the tarmac behind him. Unable to control the car, he plowed straight into a steel streetlamp and came to a jarring stop. His grill smashed, the reporter's head snapped into the steering wheel. He saw stars.

Captain Hazzard breathed an oath as all went blank in his mind, because Crawley has stopped sending, stopped receiving. Something had gone wrong! It was as though a switch on a radio had been turned off.

Back in the coupe, Crawley, blood trickling down his forehead, raised his fedora and saw the villainous second gray car whiz pass. It was moving up behind the unsuspecting patrol cruiser. Crawley saw the tripod crackling with another deadly charge and then succumbed to the pain in his head. He slumped over the wheel unconscious.

The hand of Captain Hazzard dropped to an inter-office telephone. He snatched the instrument up, barked a swift order:

"Tell Randall to warm the up Z2!"

He slammed the instrument down. In ten quick strides he crossed the room and yanked a door open, walked down a short passage and through another door made of case-hardened molybdenum steel. He passed by a glass-partitioned office where focused young men huddled over long desks, passed a machine shop where other men were working, and a laboratory where white-coated chemists stood quietly in front of instrument-strewn tables. He crossed a foundry room where the latest scientific electric crucibles were mounted and where molten metal hissed.

Heads lifted as Captain Hazzard's tall, erect figure moved past. Men saluted or nodded in respectful greeting. He was the brains, the heart, the soul of one of the greatest private laboratories in the world. Loved as a close friend by the men around him, his word in this whole, vast, busy building was law.

At one particular door, Hazzard stopped and peered inside.

Leading a group of white-jacketed researchers was a bald man with steel-rimmed glasses resting on the edge of his nose. Hearing the door open, he looked up and smiled. "Kevin?"

Professor Washington MacGowen, renowned physicist, was a life-long friend and mentor. Thus his familiarity in addressing Hazzard by his Christian name. Like his employer, Wash MacGowen also possessed strong ESP talents. He immediately sensed his friend's concern.

"Trouble?"

"Crawley seems to have tripped over something that may require our attention. I want the team assembled in one hour!"

MacGowen nodded, waving his clipboard in salute. "You got it, kid. They'll be here if I have to carry them."

That taken care of, Hazzard continued down another passage, stepped into a small automatic elevator that shot him up to the roof of the plant. The hum of a powerful airplane motor warming up filled the night air. The water of Long Island Sound gleamed close at hand. The plane itself was standing on a catapult, such as are mounted on the decks of battle cruisers.

It was a single-seater amphibian with twin pontoons, retractable landing wheels and a giant radial motor of six-hundred horsepower. Because the main section was an oval constructed from a transparent see-through plastic polymer, the craft resembled a giant egg with a propeller attached to its wide end.

A tall, grave young man in the cockpit was watching the temperature gauge intently. He stepped out and saluted as Captain Hazzard approached.

"She's almost ready, sir," Tyler Randall said.

"Stand by to release me," Hazzard replied.

He got into the narrow cockpit, adjusted flying helmet and safety belt, watched the temperature gauge creep up. In thirty seconds, he raised a gloved hand and Randall pressed a button.

There was a dull explosion, a hiss of compressed gases. The catapult boom swung forward and literally hurled the amphibian out into space away from the roof.

It shot across the water, sailed in a long trajectory, dipping down till the motor burst into a full song of throaty power. Then it lifted, banked, climbed into the night sky on its silver wings and whining steel propeller.

Hazzard made the ten miles to New York's waterfront in exactly three minutes. His plane banked high over the city, shot down like a bolt from the heavens, came to rest on the river close to the stern of the *Liberty*. He taxied into the slip, threw a dockhand a rope, made his plane fast and climbed up a ladder.

Radio police cars were gathered around the three dead men.

Cops formed a stalwart human barricade. They bristled when Captain Hazzard pushed through the crowd of curious people that had gathered. Jim Chambers, the inspector of detectives, recognized him and nodded. The police opened a path to led him through.

Inspector Chambers said: "This a hellish business, Captain Hazzard. Five men have been murdered, and the criminals have got away."

"Five?"

"Yes. These three poor chaps here and two officers in the pursuing radio car. They were knocked out the same way as these fellows. An electric ray or something. A car sneaked up behind them with a tripod gadget on it and lined them in a death zone with the car ahead."

"What about a reporter named Crawley?" asked Hazzard tensely.

"He was trying to follow the killers, too, Captain. He must have got nervous and lost control of his car. He swerved and hit a lamp post. They've taken him to the hospital with a concussion. I think he'll pull through all right."

Captain Hazzard breathed more easily. But his face was masklike in its harshness as he looked down at the three dead men. The blueness of his eyes had given way to a wintry gray.

Morgue attendants were preparing to take the bodies away on stretchers. Hazzard looked down at the still figure of the strange stowaway.

The top detective said: "It'll be hard now to find out who he was, Captain. We've been through his clothing. Nothing there to identify him. And look at his face! I doubt that he will ever be identified. His own mother wouldn't know him."

Hazzard nodded, bent down and examined the dead man. He took it for granted that the police had searched the clothing thoroughly. But something might have been overlooked. And suddenly, Hazzard's hand darted to the corpse's thick hair. His fingers slipped through, snatched at a tiny object. It was a rolled-up cylinder fastened by fiber to several strands of hair close to the scalp. The light end of it had attracted his attention.

He swiftly palmed the cylinder. Then he rose, asking Chambers the name of the hospital where William Crawley had been taken.

The inspector offered to lend Hazzard a police car, but Captain Hazzard declined. He passed outside the circle of cops, slipped through the crowd to pause at the edge of it under a street lamp. With taut fingers he unrolled the tiny cylinder. It was a strange message to find on such a man in such a place.

Printed in inked letters on tissue-thin parchment, it read:

> *The poison of red ant bites is filling my brain. The Jewel Men are close behind me. Spies of the Phoenix are waiting along the coast. Even if I can stow away aboard some ship and reach New York, I won't be safe from them. That's why I've written this to put in my hair. Maybe they won't find it when they kill me, and maybe somebody else will. If so, tell Mary Parker that her father and some of his party are still alive at N. Lat. 15.10., W. Long. 89.27. They are prisoners of the Phoenix. The others who tried to escape with me were killed. It would have been better if they'd got me, too.*
>
> *Signed...John Roan*

Hazzard read it through twice, then a sudden sense of uneasiness made him close his fingers over the parchment and whirl around. But he wasn't quite quick enough to see the furtive men on the roof of the empty store building who, through the achromatic lenses of a powerful prism monocular, had got the message by reading it over Hazzard's shoulder.

Hazzard made an impatient gesture, feeling that something was wrong. Then he strode to a telephone booth, grabbed a big directory and began thumbing through its pages looking for the address of Mary Parker.

CHAPTER TWO

The Whistling Devil

Hazzard found the address, and a swift taxi sped him on his way. At the edge of town, in one of a row of big brick houses, an aged maidservant answered his quick tug on an old-fashioned bell.

"I'm sorry for the lateness of the hour," Hazzard apologized, seeing the woman's consternation at greeting a stranger so late at night. "But it is imperative that I talk with your mistress."

"It's alright, Molly," a voice sounded from inside the house. "You may let the gentleman in."

Giving a cold-shouldered grumble, the maid opened the door wide. Stepping past her into the hallway, Captain Hazzard saw a beautiful golden-haired girl standing as straight and tall as some exotic statue. Though wearing a conservative dress, her figure was voluptuous. She had curved red lips, humid eyes, heart-shaped features. Her expression showed that she recognized him, but was puzzled at his visit.

When he reached her side, he said in a quiet voice: "You know me, don't you, Miss Parker?"

"Yes." Her dark blue eyes roamed his face with a mixture of awe and curiosity. "I've heard of you, seen your picture often. You travel all over the earth. You're a great aviator, an explorer, a scientist – a man who sometimes helps people in trouble. But" – her voice shook uneasily–"something extraordinary must have happened to bring you to my house. Tell me, has it anything to do with my father?"

He nodded gravely, looking into her eyes. "Yes."

"Oh!" The clear, rich coloring of her cheeks began to fade. She came closer, her bosom heaving, laid her hand on his arm. "Don't be afraid to speak the truth, Captain Hazzard. What have you heard from him? Is...he..."

For an answer, Hazzard took the thick parchment from his pocket and held it out. He watched her carefully as she read the brief message. He saw her face grow strained. Her eyes lifted to his and there was stark fear in them.

"Where did you get this?" She asked. "Please, tell me everything you know."

Hazzard took her arm and guided her to the sofa in the middle of the room. Once they were seated, he told her about the stowaway with the hideous face who had been slain by the weird Death Curtain.

Her cheeks turned paler. "John Roan was one of my father's men," she explained breathlessly. "What could have happened to him? And who...who is this man whom he calls the Phoenix?"

Captain Hazzard shook his head. "You may be able to help me piece this puzzle together. What was your father doing in Central America?"

"You know he was down there then?" asked Mary Parker in surprise.

Hazzard indicated the figures of latitude and longitude in the note. "Those tell the story, Miss Parker. That compass point is somewhere on the frontier between Guatemala and Honduras, close to the Espiritu Santo mountain range."

She dropped her eyes for a moment, then raised them, and looked deeply into his piercing blue-gray orbs. "I promised my father I wouldn't tell anyone where he'd gone or what he was doing," she said. "But I can talk to you, trust you, and I've got to have help now that my father is in some kind of terrible danger."

The lovely young woman took a second to sip from a glass of water on the coffee table before resuming her tale. "My father is an engineer who has been interested for many years in mining properties down in Central America. He has a partner living down there, a clever metallurgist named Kurt Gordon. Gordon and father work together extracting ores.

"Two months ago, father went down to Guatemala with a small group of experts to see Gordon about the development of some big deposits of platinum. They didn't have much capital. Rival mining companies would have tried to beat Dad to it if they'd got wind of it. That's why the thing had to be kept secret. But now..." she broke off, and tears glistened in her eyes.

"How long has it been since you've heard from him?" asked Hazzard, trying to distract the poor girl.

"Four weeks. I've radioed both father and Mr. Gordon, and they couldn't be located. I didn't know what else to do. But now that I know father's whereabouts, hadn't I better ask the governments of Guatemala and Honduras to help me? Couldn't I cable our American consulates in those countries?"

Captain Hazzard didn't answer for a moment. He was trying to guess what was behind this weirdly murderous organization that reached from the tropical jungles of Central America to the crowded streets of New York. Presently he said:

"This is big, Miss Parker. Something that must be handled with kid gloves. I've told you what happened to Roan. We don't want to do anything that will put your father in greater danger. If you asked the help of those Central American governments and they should blunder..."

"Of course, you're right!" Fear darkened the girl's eyes again. "Whatever happens ...whoever this Phoenix is...I must save my father. Captain Hazzard...couldn't you...would you consider the possibility of organizing an expedition to help me rescue him? I'll do anything I can. I have some money..."

He made an impatient gesture. "I intended to help you when I came."

"Then..."

"Wait!" Captain Hazzard tensed suddenly and lifted his head. He looked around the room in which they were sitting, and his nostrils flared. The blueness in his eyes gave way to the slaty gray. A deep instinctive sense of danger had come to him like a sinister psychic whisper, tingling his nerves.

He got up and began to move about the room uneasily, peering, prying, like a savage trying to find spoor. Mary Parker watched him silently with curious bewilderment. He came to a stop abruptly in front of a big bay window from which, when the drapes were open, one could command a view of the front stoop of the house.

Hazzard peeled back the drapes slightly and stared. The muscles under the tanned skin of his face went rigid.

Mary Parker came and stood beside him. She too stared for a moment, then lifted a trembling hand to her mouth in horror. "It's crepe!" she gasped, identifying the strands visible beneath light over the front entrance. "Black crepe! It's hanging on the door of this house as if someone were dead!"

"It wasn't there," said Hazzard, "when I arrived."

She gave a shudder. "Can it... Do you suppose it means that Father's dead?"

Hazzard shook his head. "It means something else," he surmised, "something quite different. It means that the men who killed John Roan knew about that message and know that I came here. It means they intend now to kill us both."

The tragic look on the girl's face vanished. Personal danger didn't shock her so much as fear of her father's fate. Hazzard felt a quick glow of admiration for her nerve.

He pulled her away from the window, drew the drapes, and stood for a moment thinking. His psychic feeling of menace was like a chill fog now. They were in deadly danger, and he knew it, but he didn't know from what direction the thing would strike.

A noise interrupted him, the sound of a car drawing up outside. Hazzard thrust his fingers under his coat and grasped the butt of the heavy army Colt automatic he wore in a shoulder holster. He listened and heard feet scraping to the stoop.

The bell rang loudly in the still house, stirring echoes, but Molly, Mary Parker's maid, didn't show any signs of coming to answer it.

Keeping his hand on the Colt, Captain Hazzard motioned the girl back and strode to the door himself. He stood wide-legged, his young face grim, drew the lock back and opened it.

A man in a gray uniform, wearing a visored cap, and holding a white slip of paper stood there. He looked at the gun in Hazzard's hand and swallowed hard. A big black truck was drawn up at the curb. The man said: "I don't want no trouble, pal. Is this the home of a Miss Mary Parker?"

When Hazzard nodded, the man, still watching the pistol, held out the slip of paper. "Ask her to sign this please, and let me know where she want's em."

"Wants what?" asked Hazzard.

"The two caskets. We're making a rush delivery after receiving cash payment as per instructions. Will I have 'em put downstairs or up?"

Icy prickles ran along Captain Hazzard's back. But his face was masklike, inscrutable. It was plain to him that this man in uniform was genuine; a dupe merely carrying out orders for a quick delivery of two coffins which someone else had bought. Hazzard said quietly: "Bring them in. Take them right to the drawing-room. "Holstering his .45, he went back to Mary Parker and spoke soothingly. "Don't be frightened. Our friends are enlarging their little joke. Now they've presented us with our caskets."

Hands folded under her amble bosom, she stood wide-eyed, silent, stricken as the boxes were carried in. Hazzard had them placed by the window. There was a bleak, hard smile on his face, like sunlight flashing over steel. He looked to see that both coffins were empty, signed the receipt, then dismissed the men.

The macabre black boxes so close at hand were mute reminders that they were marked for the same dread fate.

Hazzard asked : "Where is your maid's room?"

Mary Parker's hand clutched his wrist, claw-like in its tenseness.

"You're right! We must find Molly! She should have answered that doorbell."

They went down the old-fashioned, narrow stairway that led to the kitchen and the servant's quarters. His big army Colt once again in his hand, at the ready.

It was he who first caught sight of the crumpled, pitiful body of the gray-haired maid. She lay on her back on the kitchen table, glazed eyes aimed at the ceiling. There was a wire wrapped around her neck and tied in the back. Her tongue stuck out of her open mouth, her last scream a silent one as her assailant had strangled her from behind.

Mary Parker gave a sobbing sigh when she glimpsed the body and fell on her knees beside it. "Oh, Molly! Who would do such a thing to an innocent soul like this?"

Captain Hazzard didn't answer as he crouched next to her, his every nerve alert to their predicament. He understood something that the girl had failed to grasp in her sorrow. Molly's wanton murder meant that some of the against of the Phoenix were already in the house.

Even as the thought came, there was a faint sound of movement in the dark doorway beside the stairs that led to the servant's bedroom. Hazzard's hand flicked out, flung Mary Parker forward, sent her sprawling flat on the floor, and then dropped himself. He rolled over and over with the snapping suddenness of a tempered spring released.

Bullets followed him, beating a tattoo along the floor at his heels, like the fangs of Death snapping for his life. Chunks of linoleum flew into the air behind him. The snout of a sub-machine gun with a cylindrical silencer on it gleamed in that black doorway beside the stairs. And a man's eyes gleamed above the barrel.

It seemed impossible that the assassin could miss. He was turning the snarling gun on its axis, hosing bullets at Captain Hazzard. And the wall of the kitchen was directly in front of Hazzard, barring further movement.

But before he reached it, even as he was rolling over and over, Captain Hazzard's fingers flashed down to his belt, flashed up again

"Bullets beat a tattoo along the floor at his heels, like the fans of Death snapping for his life."

with something in them. His wrist snapped out. The air was filled suddenly with sparkling pellets.

Drops of diphenoloxide enclosed in eggshell-thin glass rained at the feet of the gunman, broke open, filled the air with drifting, smarting fumes. The machine gunner choked and cried out, his eyes streaming. His weapon ripped plaster from the ceiling as he tried in vain to center its sights on Captain Hazzard.

Hazzard was up in an instant. He turned, bounded across the ruined kitchen floor, ducked sideways to avoid the wildly swinging stream of slugs. His gun muzzle barked once and his shot, at near point-blank range, took off the killer's skull in a spray of blood and gore. As the dead man fell backwards, his sub-caliber weapon fell out of his lifeless hands. Hazzard snatched it up. Then he helped the girl to her feet and together they ran to the back door that led to the garden.

It was unlocked, half open. But caution stayed Hazzard before he bolted through. Caution made him fling the door wide, let his shadow precede him, and freeze in his tracks.

It was well he did so. There was a sudden snapping hiss in the darkness as lead from other silenced sub-calibers converged on the spot where his body would have been.

The slugs came close. They bit at the door frame and forced Hazzard back. There was a grim smile on his lips. He hadn't really expected that there would be an easy way out. Left to himself, he might have played a game of death with those men outside. But there was the girl to consider.

He closed the door quickly, snapped a bolt into place, put the lights out and caught Mary Parker's hand. He led her through the gloom of the kitchen, around the body of Molly, towards the stairs. She was sobbing softly.

He had marked the location of the stairway, and he went to it easily, as though it had been light. Darkness held no terrors for him. He had lived in the dark too long to fear it now. When he reached the upstairs hallway, he switched out the bulb there, left Mary Parker for a moment, and strode to the front door. He opened it and looked up and down the street cautiously.

A gray car was parked a few yards along the block. Metal rods gleamed on the top of it like the antennae of a huge, malignant scorpion poised to strike. Hazzard recognized the car immediately from the mental images Crawley had sent him earlier.

On the other side of the house, a hundred yards away, a second car with a duplicate tripod was parked. Between them, already visible, was a faint aura of eerie luminescence.

Hazzard gritted his teeth. He and Mary Parker were trapped.

Guns waited in the yard behind them. In front, ready to sweep them into oblivion, was that weird, pulsating curtain of unholy death.

CHAPTER THREE

Stairway To Hell

He could feel the strange influences of it even as he looked. Dizziness filled him. He raised the submachine gun, but his fingers shook so that he couldn't aim it. He wasn't afraid. It was the unseen, unknown force of that weird, deathly light striking the cells of his body that made him shake. A few yards closer, he knew, could spell certain doom.

He backed up, shut the door quickly, and saw Mary Parker coming towards him along the hall. Her face was white. She said through tight lips: "There's someone moving upstairs. I just heard footsteps."

Hazzard heard them too, knew that the agents of the Phoenix were closing in.

Mary Parker's voice was a dry, taut whisper: "The telephone! Can't we call the police?"

He went to it, but found as he had expected that the line was dead – cut.

He could send a mental message through space that would summon his own assistants. But he dismissed all thought of that. To call them without giving full information of what they would find would only be leading them to slaughter. And even Captain Hazzard couldn't pretend to transmit telepathically details of the complex situation he now faced.

His only course was to fight it out alone.

"There must be a skylight," he said, looking upwards. "They've come across the tops of the roofs and broken through it. Now they're coming down."

"Yes," the girl confirmed. "All the houses on this block are the same height."

Hazzard asked quickly: "The one next door, on the right – who lives in it?"

"No one. It's vacant."

"Then we've got to go up." His voice was vibrant. He eyes held an anticipation of battle.

"But they're waiting there now!" she whispered back, thinking he was being recklessly foolhardy. "They'll surely catch and kill us."

He didn't answer. Experience on the wild frontiers of the world had taught him that all life is a gamble when death is close. And Hazzard still had some dice of his own to toss on Fate's table.

His belt was strong and wide and made of pliant leather. It had many small pouches, apparently for cartridges. But the compact spaces held a score of objects other than shells. In them he carried some of the gadgets that were the product of his inventive skills, articles he had turned out during his spare time in the laboratory on Long Island.

Hazzard chose a small, greenish, oval-shaped object with blunt excrescences on it. It looked like an enlarged bronze model of some sort of scarab. But the blunt points had tiny holes in them. Hazzard called it his Whistling Devil.

He touched a button on one end of it and a faint sputter sounded in the strange thing's interior. Acid began to eat through a tinfoil outer shell. In a moment, when it touched another acid, a gas would be generated and pressure would build up.

He tossed it into the room with the two coffins, then pulled the girl cautiously towards the stairs.

A minute passed, and then hell seemed to break loose in that darkened chamber. A fiend appeared to be whipping itself into a stark raving fury. A shrill screech sounded as gas shot through a whistling vent. The screech mounted. Other screeches joined it. Gas under terrific pressure in the bronze jacket spurted through a dozen whistling vents. The force of it pushed the thing around the room like a whirlwind. It banged into chairs, hit the wall, leaped toward the ceiling, screeching, jumping, clattering.

In the midst of this terrible din, Hazzard took Mary Parker's trembling hand and drew her up the stairs. He knew that the Devil's noise would drown out the creak of their steps. The men waiting above would hear nothing except that startling, nerve-racking sound below.

Submachine gun held tightly against his right side as he made his way up, Hazzard's eyes stabbed the gloom. At the first landing, he suddenly thrust the weapon into the girl's hands and pushed her behind him. He leaped forward, hurling himself like a projectile on a dim human form he had spotted straight ahead. A man was standing at the top of the stairs, gun in hand, eyes wide in alarm, trying to make out what the fearful racket below was all about.

He saw Hazzard and tried to raise his pistol. Hazzard knocked it form his hand, then caught him around the waist in a football tackle and lifted him bodily. The man struggled, yelled. Without hesitation, Hazzard threw him over the bannister in a savage, lightning heave that sent the fellow hurtling to the floor below. The gunman landed on his head. His body made a thud when it hit the floor, no sound came above the wail of the Whistling Devil.

Hazzard drew Mary Parker on to the second-story hall, relieving of her the big Thompson machine gun. He set it down gently against the wall. There he paused, peered up and caught dim movement somewhere between him and the glass skylight of the stairwell. Downstairs, the sound of the Devil was growing fainter now. The gas was almost exhausted. Soon the creak of the stairs under them would be heard. It was time to toss another of his dice.

He put down the machine gun and whipped a handkerchief from his pocket, turning to Mary Parker and whispering close to her ear: "I'm going to tie this over your eyes and nose."

"What for?" Her voice was a thin gasp of fear. The delicate rose scent of her perfume teased his nose.

"Smoke bomb," he said, ignoring the sweet smell of her. He

placed the handkerchief over her face, knotted it in back. Then he drew a cylinder from his belt containing a combination of carbon tetrachloride, sand, zinc dust and magnesium. It was a miniature smoke pot having the same chemical basis as the type used in wartime to hide military ground maneuvers.

He pressed a spark lighter, hurled the cylinder up the stairwell to the floor above. In a moment, even the dim glow of the skylight was shut off. Smoke so thick it seemed to have solid substance mushroomed out, filling the whole house. It rolled down the stairs in a stygian cloud, floated up in a sable curtain. Through it, Hazzard faintly heard the oaths of startled men.

Hazzard snatched up the machine gun and pressed it against his side once more. He took a deep breath, closed his eyes. Death might still strike through the smoke, for those above had more guns like this. They couldn't see, but they might decide to shoot at random, lay a barrage of lead that would spell destruction.

That was a chance he had to take. He made Mary Parker walk behind him, holding her fingers in his left hand and climbing quickly, keeping the bannister on his right. Close to the second floor, Mary Parker stumbled as her high heels caught in the stair carpet. She gave a choking cry. Instantly, there was movement above them.

Hazzard pulled her down beside him in a crouch seconds before bullets snarled over their heads. He couldn't see the flash of guns. The silencers on the sub-caliber weapons almost deadened the sound of the shots. It was eerie having silent lead come at him out of that black cloud. But he heard the deathly whine of the lead slugs zipping past his head, felt the wind they made.

His own finger pressed the curved trigger of the gun he had procured from the slain killer in the kitchen. With a jerk, the barrel spit death at his unseen foes. He heard a vicious slap as his bullets struck, heard the scream of a man mortally wounded.

A human form came stumbling down the stairs, struck his shoulder a glancing blow, and caromed on behind him.

Mary Parker, flattened against the steps, barely missed being hit by the falling body. Another gun hissed to life. Cold fear clutched Hazzard's heart – fear for Mary Parker's life. He fired another salvo at the shooter above until it grew quiet.

There was an audible click as the weapon in his hand went silent, too, the drum empty.

He still had his automatic, but he wanted to save its shells. They might be needed later. Even if they reached the roof, there would be more killers waiting for them.

Holding the sub-caliber gun as a club, Hazzard sprang up, pulling the girl with him. A man collided with him, and Hazzard struck. There was groan followed by a thud. Hazzard plunged on through the smoke cloud, reached the top hallway. A cool draft told him that the open skylight was just ahead.

But he could see no stars. The black pall funneled upward, hiding the sky. But it would thin presently. Then eyes in the surrounding darkness would see. Crouching men on other roofs would fling lead at them. There might be a – of the Phoenix's killers around them for all Hazzard knew. They would guess soon enough that he and the girl had reached the roof. They would figure on a running flight along the housetops as the obvious way of escape.

But Hazzard never did the obvious. He moved to the right, to the roof of the empty house next door. Here he stopped again. The billowing smoke still hid them. He had a few seconds in which to work. His hands felt for the skylight.

"You're not going down there?" questioned Mary Parker, her voice muffled by the handkerchief.

"Yes. We are."

"But you said their car was parked just out front. You said the death curtain –"

"That's why I'm doing it. They won't expect us. They'll think we're running."

He didn't say that he had another plan in mind. He drew a thin hacksaw blade from his belt, slipped it under the skylight cover, and cut the hooks. In a moment he raised it softly, stepped in and guided the girl along. He peeled the handkerchief from her face.

"Hurry!" he said.

They moved down the stairs of the dark, empty house like a pair of fugitive ghosts. Hazzard peered under a drawn shade at street level and saw the killer's gray car standing directly outside. The faint aura of the death curtain was still visible, but only in front of the hair-like antenna. If he could take those men in the parked vehicle by surprise...

But he could see a head on the front seat now. And there must be one or more men in back. Hazzard turned to the girl. "I'm going to open the door and rush them. You stay here and watch. If I beckon, you come running."

Before she could protest, he flung the door wide and went down the steps, shooting. His first bullet glanced off the car's engine hood. The man behind the wheel, the vicious faced killer with hyena teeth, turned and a gun came magically to his fingers.

Flame lanced and lead brushed close to Captain Hazzard. But Hazzard's next two shots caught the villain in the chest. They seemed to lift Hyena-face in the car seat and batter him to the floorboards.

Other bullets streaked from the rear of the car from a curtained side window. Without breaking his oncoming charge, Hazzard fired repeatedly until spidery cracks appeared in the shatter-proof glass. The gun flame behind the glass suddenly ceased. Taking a desperate chance, Hazzard stopped, turned and motioned to Mary Parker.

She didn't hesitate an instant. Her nerve raised his respect for her. She came down the stoop with her eyes wide and her golden hair flying.

Hazzard held his breath for fear she might not make it. He surveyed the yard and the street looking for the rest of the gang. Suddenly, chips danced close beside the running girl on the sidewalk as cupronickel rounds whipped at her feet from the guns on the roof above. Hazzard sent several shots into the air providing cover. Then she was close to the open door of the sedan. Hazzard heaved out the dead driver, pulled the girl in and took the wheel.

Luckily the motor was running. In a moment the gray car started to roll. But that other car, the one with the same antennae on it, was parked ahead. Men leaned out of it, firing at them. Hazzard hit the brakes, backed and twisted the wheel hard. Fat tires bounced up over the sidewalk and made a desperate turn with lead crashing into the car's chassis.

He got the headlights pointed in the opposite direction and pressed his foot on the gas. There was plenty of power under the long gray hood. The car bolted ahead like a racehorse given the whip. But the second car behind was moving to give them chase.

Mark Parker crouched beside him, her cheeks flaming with excitement. He was glad they were near the suburbs, where traffic would be negligible at this late hour. He could hold the motor wide open, gamble on his driving skills to get them away.

He sped through quiet, deserted streets, whirled onto an open highway, braked daringly and flung the big automobile on a hairpin turn into another road that ran off at a right angle from it.

A quick glance in the rearview mirror told him their pursuers were still on their tail. A hail of bullets from behind glanced off the gray car's roof, bit into its body, threatened to tear its rubber tires to shreds. And suddenly, a dull explosion sounded a few from their backs.

Hazzard looked back over his right shoulder. Lead had found a mark somewhere in the strange mechanism that made the veil of deathly light. Following that dull report, smoke commenced pouring out of both side doors, and he could see flickering light around the edges of the shade that covered the glass behind the driver's compartment.

The speeding gray car was on fire. But to stop now, even to slow up beside the road, meant being mowed down by the gunmen in the second car. Keep moving or stop, either way spelled doom, and Hazzard had no other options.

CHAPTER FOUR

Expedition To Nowhere

Mary Parker was gamely silent even when the shade began burning and the window behind them gave out a sinister snap. Hazzard could feel the heat of it on his neck and he glanced back ascertain the fire's progress.

The shade had fallen. For the first time, he looked into the car's interior and got a glimpse of the man his bullets had felled back at the house. The murderer of John Roan and four others was now a corpse himself. A horrible human torch with head lolling and hair and clothes ablaze. His thin-lipped features made a ghastly grinning mask in the light of the flames.

A black box holding part of the mechanism of the weird death curtain was also burning. It was out of this that the hottest flames were leaping. Its deadly power was destroyed, but by an ironic twist of fate, it still menaced their lives.

Hazzard's face was strained. His knuckles curved whitely over the black rim wheel. The car had become a seething comet. If they stayed in it much longer, they would be swept on to a fiery finish.

He looked for some way out. All hope of saving the death curtain mechanism for investigation had vanished. His only thought now was to save their lives. The ignition would burn through presently, the engine would go dead and the car would stop by itself. They would then be easy targets for the armed men behind.

Hazzard raced on a few seconds longer, until he spotted a field of tall, dry weed stems caught in his headlight beams. He felt a sudden surge of hope. The night wind was bending the vegetation toward them. A stiff gale was sweeping the stalks almost flat. There was a flimsy, weathered fence surrounding the field.

Hazzard called to the girl to hold on tight. He twisted toward the field with sudden violence. The gray car nearly flipped over as it careened about on two wheels. It left the road, bounced over a ditch and struck the wooden fence at a sharp angle.

Rails splintered and the windshield was cracked by a chunk of flying debris. Hazzard brought the sedan around in a wide curve straight into the wind and plunged through the dry weed beds. The engine died suddenly, the headlights winking out. But the fire behind them made a golden glow like a giant torch.

"Jump!" Hazzard literally threw the girl from the seat. She fell on her silken knees in the coarse grass. Now that the car had stopped moving, the flames licked forward into the driver's seat. The glass behind it burst and the fire reached for Hazzard even as he jumped free.

As he hit the ground in a practiced shoulder roll, he heard the squealing tires of the killer's car in the road. Over his shoulder, he saw its headlights goggling as it turned and came through the new opening in the fence. He kept Mary Parker from rising as lead cut the stalks over their heads.

The killer's vehicle raced toward them. Hazzard had his automatic out and was shooting, but he was facing men armed with superior firepower. His few bullets couldn't stop their assault.

His hope centered on something else.

Then it happened just as he had envisioned! The pluming flames that the wind beat back from the burning auto caught the dry alfalfa. The grass went up like tinder. It fanned out before the gale on both sides, making a scorching barrier of flame and smoke that bore down

*"The glass behind it burst and the fire reached for
Hazzard even as he jumped free."*

on the attackers. This was what Hazzard had planned when he had driven the burning car into the field.

"Now!" He pulled the girl to her feet and drew her after him in front of the shield wall of fire. They reached the other side of the field and Hazzard heard the shrill whine of a laboring motor as the killer's car backed up in the soft dirt.

There was a grim, tight smile on his face. He had used the fire which their shots had set to start another conflagration, which had in turn stopped them. He hurried with the girl across empty lots and found the road that led to the city. Twenty minutes of fast walking brought them to a suburban street where he was able to hail a passing cab.

"Whitestone Avenue, College Point. The Hazzard Laboratories," he directed the cabbie.

The hack started when he recognized his distinguished passenger's face. Those piercing eyes, that hawklike nose and neat mustache and rugged chin had been pictured often in the papers. He touched his cap respectfully and said, "Yes, sir, Captain. Whatever you say!"

No sooner had they started down the street when the wail of oncoming sirens sounded. Seconds later two firetrucks going in the opposite direction passed them and Hazzard knew they were on their way to deal with the burning field. He made a mental note to later recompense the owner of that property for any damages his actions may have caused. He was a man of conscience and would not stand by and allow innocent bystanders to suffer as a result of his campaign against the forces of crime.

Hazzard leaned back with eyes closed as the cab slid through the night. Mary Parker looked at him anxiously as if he were ill. His face was rapt, trance-like. But something about his appearance awed her, made her keep still.

She didn't know that his mind was concentrating, sending out telepathic impulses of energy that sped through space ahead of them.

When they reached the laboratory complex on College Point, lights sparkled and several massive buildings seemed to hum with activity. Hazzard pointed out a big flying field to the right and a several giant hangars. Men in denim were swinging the tail of a huge two-motored monoplane around on a dolly. Skilled mechanics were walking along the torpedo-shaped fuselage toward the giant motors. The ship crouched on its fat airwheels, facing the field lights like a colossal moth ready to take wing.

A young, keen-faced man stood by the watchman at the hangar gate. He came forward eagerly when the cab with Captain Hazzard and the girl rolled up. At the sight of her, the fellow's interest perked up with very charming smile.

"I got your orders, Captain. You wanted the *Silver Bullet* tuned and made ready. Randall got here five minutes ago and is giving her a final system check. You're going south tonight?"

The girl stiffened in surprise. Captain Hazzard hadn't stopped along the way to use a phone. She didn't see how he could have transmitted any orders to anyone. But Hazzard made no explanation.

"This is one of my assistants, Miss Parker. Doctor Martin Tracey. He's going with us. You can tell him everything. I'm going to leave him with you for a while."

Tracey stepped up and bowed, his handsome tanned face cracked into a friendly grin. "Thank you, Captain." He took Mary Parker's arm and began to escort her to adjacent lab.

"Captain," she said, holding up her hand to interrupt his departure. In it was a crumpled piece of paper. "I believe this could be of use to you."

Hazzard turned and reached for the paper with a puzzled look on his face.

"It's the city registration for the gray car," Mary Parker explained. "I took it from the glovebox during the chase."

"Brains as well as beauty," Martin Tracey commented to his boss. "You've found a winner this time, Captain."

"Indeed I have," Hazzard concurred, shoving the registration form into his shirt pocket. There was a warm glint of unabashed appreciation in his blue eyes. "Thank you, Miss Parker. Now if you'll excuse me, we've much to get ready before sunrise."

As Mary Parker took Tracey's offered arm, Hazzard was already twenty feet ahead. He went to his private offices and found another of his assistants waiting. The tall, bald-headed man of forty whose shrewd eyes were owlish behind steel-rimmed spectacles was seated at one of the many desks in the main reception area.

Washington MacGowen, called "Wash" for short, was a mathematical physicist and one of the most skillful laboratory technicians in the entire world. He was also Hazzard's close friend and mentor.

He came to his feet as Hazzard entered. His face was long and solemn. "I've been worried about you, Kevin," he muttered angrily. "You've been in danger, fighting a group of thugs who tried their best to kill you in some peculiar way. Why didn't you call some of us for help?"

Hazzard smiled red-faced. Wash, too, was able to receive and transmit telepathic messages. He was among the few hand-picked men who knew Hazzard's secrets. Along with Martin Tracey and William Crawley, Hazzard had given him the card test for telepathy and clairvoyance when he'd first come to Hazzard Labs to work.*

-----*AUTHOR'S NOTE* *

This is the test worked out by Doctor Rhine of Duke University. Twenty-five cards are used with five different symbols; a circle, a square, a cross, a star and a wave design consisting of three lines. The subject reads the symbols without seeing them, or attempts to do so, and, by a count based on the law of mathematical probability, they unerringly tell whether or not he is gifted with psychic perception.

Hazzard soberly replied, "I didn't call you, Wash, because you're too valuable to lose. And you'd have been killed if you'd come to my assistance." He then proceeded to describe the strange action of the curtain of death.

Wash nodded his bald head and looked still more solemn when Hazzard had finished. "If I could only get a look at that thing, Kevin, I might be able—"

"The apparatus caught fire when bullets struck it," said Hazzard. He quickly swept up the nearest phone and put in a call to the police commissioner of New York. When the commissioner answered, he was not at all happy about being roused in the wee hours of the morning. When Hazzard identified himself, the commissioner calmed down. He had known the adventurer for many years and knew he would never make such a call unless it was for a matter of utmost importance.

He stopped fuming and told Hazzard to continue.

"Your men have found a burning car in a lot at the edge of town by this time. It is what caused the field there to burn. There's a dead man in it. I killed him. I'm not interested in the body. But I am interested in the car. If you'll have it rushed to my compound as soon as it is cool enough to handle, I might be able to give you some information on those death-curtain murders at the harbor. I'll hand the car back as soon as my people have finished with it."

He listened for a moment, and then taking out the slip of paper Mary Parker had retrieved from the gray car and read off the name and address printed there. "I believe the rest of the gang that escape in the second car may be still be at this address. If you move fast, you might be able to round them all up. Right, exactly. Thank you, Commissioner."

Hazzard snapped the instrument down and turned to Wash. "The commissioner is agreeable. If they get the car out here soon enough, you may be able to go over it before we fly."

"Then you plan to take me with you?" There was sudden eagerness in Wash's voice.

Hazzard nodded. "I couldn't risk leaving you behind, Wash. Before we crack this riddle, we'll need all the brains we've got. And now..." Hazzard pressed a button on the intercom box. "I have to check with Randall on the status of the *Silver Bullet*. And where's Jake Cole tonight?"

Without waiting for Wash to answer, Hazzard spoke into the inter-office amplifier that sounded in every room of the main building and even out into the hangars. "Hazzard calling. Will Jake Cole please report to my office immediately."

In response, a tall, lanky man entered Hazzard's office a few minutes later, outfitted in western regalia. Under a ten-gallon white hat he had a stiff crest of straw-blond hair, a deadpan face, ungainly hands and feet and a nose which sometime or another had been broken. Hands stuffed in the pockets of his Levis, he was chewing gum as he approached Hazzard nonchalantly without a salute or so much as a nod.

He was Jake Cole, ex-cowhand from Montana. With only a sixth-grade education, he knew nothing about science, could hardly add a column of small figures. An auto engine was a deep enigma to him. His tests with the telepathic cards had proved his extra-sensory powers nonexistent. But he had certain talents of his own. He was a wizard with a lasso. He could shoot like an Apache with rifle or six-gun, and he was one of the best trackers in the West. No man or horse could leave a trail too faint for Cole to follow.

Hazzard said, "Get your guns oiled, Jake. We're starting out for the banana republics in about two hours. I think we may see something of the jungle while down there."

"Suits me, Captain," Cole's jaws worked rhythmically. His deadpan face didn't show any emotion. But Hazzard, who could read his mind like a book, knew that the cowboy was seething with excitement. He smiled as Cole turned and shuffled off to pack up his equipment he always carried in the warmer climes.

Then Captain Hazzard began the serious business of organizing the expedition to go in search of Mary Parker's father.

A half-hour before the time set for their departure, the car in which Hazzard and Mary Parker had taken their wild ride was delivered by police escort to the gates of the complex. Wash MacGowen had the tow-truck drop the charred hulk in the garage bay of the main research facility. Once the cops were gone, he and three of his best technicians began a detailed examination of the car's interior.

Methodically, they tore out what was left of the fire-curtain mechanism, recorded measurements with micrometers, poked and pried with delicate instruments. Wash covered scratch pads with hastily sketched designs and long mathematical equations, then made his finished report to Captain Hazzard.

Like most scientists, Wash was a cautious man, not given to sensational statements or emotional moods, but Hazzard could see now that he was excited to an abnormal degree. His voice shook as he stood tensely by Hazzard's desk, peering down through steel-rimmed glasses.

"I hesitate to make positive conclusions, Kevin. But that thing does not appear to be electrical in any ordinary sense. Still, some type of electrical amplifiers may have been used. We found a socket that might have held some sort of tube for a carrier wave. Long since melted, it's impossible to be sure. Likewise, there was something that resembled a saline condenser. The rest of the contraption is mystifying.

"The rods on top aren't radio antennae. They're made of barium wrapped around a core of tungsten. The other metal we found is an alloy, molybdenum and rhodonite. I wouldn't want to be quoted, but my best guess is that this thing generated, or used, a force outside the field of everyday physics."

Hazzard nodded. "Maybe some form of molecular or atomic energy?"

"Yes, indeed, Kevin. But good heavens —"

Hazzard stood up and interrupted him. "If you'd seen the light rays as I did, felt the effect of them, and seen those poor chaps who were killed by them, you wouldn't hesitate to follow any kind of reasoning. We're up against a deadly puzzle, Wash. And the man who invented this murder weapon is either a homicidal paranoiac or a scheming criminal mastermind. We don't know who he is or anything about him. All we know is...he's going to make our trip south mighty dangerous. Now..." Hazzard glanced at his wristwatch... "it's time we were going!"

Ten minutes later, their personal gear stowed away on the magnificent flying fortress called the *Silver Bullet*, Captain Hazzard and MacGowen took their places in the spacious cabin. The airplane had a mobile lab and that was the section Wash sought out. In the main passenger cabin, Jake Cole sat chewing another wad of gum. Strapped to the seat beside him were a coiled lasso and a beautiful polished high-powered rifle. Across the spacious aisle from the cowboy, the dapper Martin Tracey helped the lovely Mary Parker strap into her seat. She was dressed in a smart tropical outfit consisting of boots, shorts and shirt of durable lightweight khaki. Tracey wore an identical outfit, but with long pants.

In the cockpit, Tyler Randall occupied the copilot's seat, where he did a pre-flight check with Captain Hazzard.

When all was ready, Tyler waved to the ground crew and the mechanics quickly stepped away. Slowly, with a deft hand on the controls, Hazzard taxied the big metal bird out of the hangar and onto his private airstrip. The rumble of the twin motors rose to a vibrant roar. The great plane quivered, then rolled forward into the wind.

The ship gathered speed, leaped into the purpling sky with a majestic thrust of unleashed power. Her silver wings canted. She left the ground so smoothly that Mary Parker didn't realize they were airborne until she saw the dwindling lights of the field and the hangars falling away.

Hazzard banked, swept out over the Sound for a few minutes, then rose higher, pointing the *Silver Bullet's* nose straight south. He climbed until the tall skyscrapers of Manhattan thrust up into the sky behind them, until Brooklyn and Queens and the Bronx spread out as on a table. He climbed higher on the wings of the wind till New York fell away, became lost in the violet haze of dawn, and the coast of New Jersey unrolled below them like a glowing bas-relief map.

Lancing pink and orange rays from the east colored the heavens over the Atlantic Ocean. It was going to be a glorious morning.

Then Randall, looking around with an airman's alertness, suddenly spoke. "There's something in the sky behind us, sir.

It seems to getting nearer. You don't suppose..."

"Yes," confirmed Hazzard. "I've been watching it for the past two minutes. It's another plane following us. Hanging right on our tail."

CHAPTER FIVE

The Sky Shark

The strange ship was a light blur in the lightening sky behind them. The dogged way it followed them made it seem sinister. It disappeared for seconds when mist intervened, then reappeared as rising sunlight glinted like jewels off its wings.

Hazzard climbed still higher and advanced the throttle. The *Silver Bullet* roared up through the dawn sky – seven thousand, eight thousand. The air grew thin and cold. Hazzard flattened, advanced the throttle still more, watched eagerly to see whether the plane behind could still keep up. It did. More than that, it was climbing for still greater altitude, getting a thousand feet above their tail.

In the cabin, the three men and Mary Parker hung on determinedly as the big plane went through its elusive gyrations. Martin Tracey saw that the girl was white-faced from obvious fear as her hands gripped the arms of her seat. He leaned over and whispered in her, "It's okay, Mary. Really. Cap's the best damn pilot in the world. He knows what he's doing up there. He'll get us through."

The girl turned to him and smiled weakly, "Thank you, Dr. Tracey."

The handsome surgeon winked mischievously, "Call me Martin, or you'll hurt my feelings."

Jake Cole didn't particularly like flying all that much himself, but he wasn't about to show his own innate worries with a civilian on board. Listening to Tracey's banter with Mary Parker, the Montana wrangler grinned to himself. Leave it to that playboy Tracey to sweet-talk a girl in the middle of an aerial duel.

While in the cockpit, a sense of real danger filled Hazzard.

He saw the blur of the other plane change its outline. He got the impression that the tail was up now, the nose down. The ship grew bigger, its superior altitude giving it increased speed. It was in a fast power dive.

Then a searchlight winked from the nose of that other craft. It stabbed across the blue-gray sky like a spectral finger, and rested on the fuselage of the *Silver Bullet*. Hazzard's plane hung between the rays of the new sun on one side and the dazzling artificial beam on the other like a moth caught between two flames.

Sparks suddenly shot from the beam of the searchlight. They were tracer bullets from a machine gun and they snarled close to Hazzard's ship. Slugs were mixed with the tracers. One snapped through the *Silver Bullet's* starboard wing.

But only one. Hazzard side-slipped away quickly. The beam of the searchlight left them. The other plane went roaring by. Hazzard got a glimpse of it. It was a small, fast, low-wing monoplane with a single motor. It was coming back now. It had the flashing speed of the fastest army pursuit job, and it seemed invincible in a dogfight of this kind. For all its sophistication and capabilities, the *Silver Bullet* could never outmaneuver the smaller ship.

But Hazzard wasn't completely without resources. He gave an order to Randall. "Raise the L.O. motor, then stand by!"

Randall reached forward and pulled a small, red lever. There was a faint grinding vibration in the ship. For a moment it lost speed as something obstructed the aerodynamic flow of the slipstream above the fuselage. Thin metal panels in the top of the *Silver Bullet* slid back. From between them a huge torpedo shaped object appeared. It rose on powerful steel supports till it was six feet above the fuselage, the narrow tip pointing backward, well above the tail assembly. There was a round vent in this end section.

"All ready, sir," announced Randall.

Hazzard threw another switch on the instrument board and the

"The other plane went roaring by. Hazzard got a glimpse of it. It was a small, fast, low-wing monoplane with a single motor. It was coming back now."

strange cigar-shaped thing began to hum a deeper note than the forward motors. It was another motor, an auxiliary rocket motor, using a mixture of liquid oxygen and high-test gasoline, and based on the same general principles as Fritz von Opel's rocket engines used successfully on cars in Germany. It was one of the many, many reasons why the *Silver Bullet* was no ordinary aircraft.*

--------*AUTHOR'S NOTE - **

In creating the first efficient rocket motor for use in airplanes, Captain Hazzard first studied the research of such experts as Valier, von Opel, Doctor Goddard, Herman Oberth and others. His success lies in the great improvement of his carburetor-type injection nozzles, through which the freezing cold liquid oxygen is fed into the combustion chamber. The main drawback of Hazzard's and all other rocket motors is their tendency to overheat.

A faint glow appeared at the tip of the vent. The glow became a blush of light, then a shooting flame, reaching back suddenly across the sky. It seemed to burn a vacuum in the air.

The pilot in the other ship must have thought he had set Hazzard's ship on fire. The powerful stream of gas shooting from the torpedo-shaped motor was like the fiery tail of a comet. It boosted the two forward motors of regular design.

The *Silver Bullet* surged forward. A hundred miles an hour was instantly added to its speed. The long stream of fiery gas streaked back across the heavens as straight as a chalk line on a blackboard. The *Silver Bullet* was on a plumb-line course for the south. No turns or quick maneuvers were possible while the rocket was engaged.

For a brief moment the hostile plane was visible in its afterglow, a dancing hornet in the giant sunbeam. But its sting was ineffectual now. It fell behind, disappearing in the mist as Hazzard's ship outdistanced it with a speed no ordinary plane could match.

Mark Parker saw the glow in the sky behind and stared with frightened eyes. Again, Martin Tracey put her fears to rest. He explained how the rocket motor functioned. The girl was quickly realizing that there was no end to the marvels Captain Hazzard was capable of producing.

With the aid of the auxiliary power unit, the *Silver Bullet* was traveling at terrific velocity now. But while the rocket motor was running, Hazzard watched the temperature dial with a wary eye. The liquid oxygen, close to minus one-hundred-ninety degrees centigrade when it was injected into the combustion chamber, soon became fearfully hot. Overheating was a constant menace.

The *Silver Bullet* roared through the night, crossing cities, counties and states as it sped southward on its strange rescue quest.

CHAPTER SIX

Morning Raid

Meanwhile, back in New York, gathered around a short-wave radio set in a seedy cold-water flat on the East Side, the four remaining members of the Phoenix's American gang listened incredulously to the report coming over the speaker. The tall man with the blue-black hair and sickly white pallor was seated in front of the wireless, manipulating the tuning dials.

"Repeat last transmission. Over, " he spoke into the stand-up microphone on the table before him. He was communicating with the pilot of the monoplane now on its way back to the city.

"How many ways you want me to say it?" the angry voice retorted. "Hazzard and his crew got away from me. Over."

"That's nuts!" the tall man cursed. "He should have been a sitting duck to your machine gun. Over."

"Yeah, well this duck didn't sit still. He had some kind of rocket jet built into that plane of his. Over."

"Rocket jet? There's no such thing. Over." The tall man chewed on an unlit cigar in his mouth. The news he was getting was also giving him a sour stomach.

"Listen, Butch, I had them all lined up in my sights when, *whammo*, just like that, the entire plane takes off like a bat out of hell going faster than any ship I've ever seen. They must be halfway to Mexico by now. Over.''

As much as he hated the news, the one called Butch had no recourse but to accept it. There was nothing else he could do, except notify the boss that Hazzard had escaped yet again and was now on his way to Secret Mountain.

"Alright. Get back to the city as fast as you can. We'll have new orders for you by then. Over and out."

"Roger that. See you in a few hours. Over and out."

With the radio silent, static filled the air around the high-quality mahogany set. Seated behind Butch on a ripped up second-hand sofa, the big man with the bloated face took off his fedora and mopped his sweaty brow with a handkerchief. His name was Anderson.

"You gonna radio the Phoenix?" he asked the tall man.

"What other choice do I got?" came the crestfallen reply.

"He's gonna be mad. Real mad."

"Maybe," Butch agreed. "But he'd be even more riled up if we didn't let him know Hazzard was on his way down there. At least by warning the boss, he's still got time to put together a real nice reception for that do-gooder boy scout."

Setting down his unlit cigar, Butch re-tuned the shortwave set and began sending out a new transmission.

"New York One, calling the Phoenix. Come in, Phoenix."

There were a few minutes of silence, and the gangster sub-chief repeated his call a second time. Finally he was rewarded with a deep, resonant voice: "This is the Phoenix, New York One. Report."

As Butch proceeded to inform his employer about the botched air attack, one of the other men in the room walked into the small square kitchen to brew a fresh pot of coffee. It had been a long night, what with the gun battle in the suburbs followed by the car chase and the narrow escape from the coppers out in the burning alfalfa field. The surviving crew had made it back to their humble hideout only hours earlier and all of them were bone-weary. The hired gun figured a fresh pot of joe would wake them all up.

He was reaching for the cabinet door over the sink counter when an outside reflection on the back window caught his attention.

Looking down into the alley behind the tenement house, he spotted several policemen moving in from the street corner with guns drawn. Another was coming out of the garage at the end of the alley where they kept the remaining gray car with the death-curtain machine. The hood knew their number was up.

"It's the cops!" he warned, racing back into the other room.

At the same time, there was a banging at the front door.

"Open up in there! Police!"

"Nobody's taking me back to the big house!" Bloated-face declared, jumping off the couch and waving his sub-machine gun.

But before he could fire a single round, the wooden door was smashed inward and Inspector James Chambers appeared in the opening, followed by half-dozen boys in blue.

"Drop it!" Chambers said. Bloated-face aimed at him and Chambers fired off two quick shots. The first caught the killer in the chest while the other went through his right eye. He fell back over the couch and slumped to the floor.

At the same time, his cohorts had also drawn their own guns and entered the melee with a barrage of shots. Chambers, seeing how small the room was, dove to the hardwood floor as hundreds of slugs filled the air. Windows shattered, walls were perforated and men on both sides caught lead in unprotected flesh. The Phoenix's crew were hardened criminals who expected no mercy from the courts and had resigned themselves to going out in a blaze of gunpowder.

In two minutes it was over. Several officers lay wounded in various spots, whereas not a sound or movement came from the outlaws. All of them were silent, in eternal repose where they had fallen. Butch, the tall leader, was stretched over the table, his head inches from the now ruined radio.

In the wispy haze of acrid gunsmoke, Inspector Chambers got to his feet and surveyed the carnage. Seeing his wounded men, he called one of his sergeants now entering from the hall, "Get an ambulance here on the double! I want those men taken care of at once!"

The veteran copper saluted and raced back out to the command radio car. As he started around the corner, Chambers called after him: "And notify the city morgue we've got business for them."

"Hell of a way to start the day, isn't it, Inspector?" William Crawley climbed over the wreckage of the front door. He looked no less hale and hearty for his own flirtation with death the night before. The only indication of that encounter was the white surgical tape wrapped around his temple, under his brown fedora.

"You can say that again," the inspector nodded, putting his .38-caliber gun back in its shoulder rig. "How's the head?"

"I'll live," the ace reporter said as he took in the aftermath of the shootout. "I could hear the gunfire out in the streets."

"Tough bunch," the top cop stated the obvious. "Senseless way to go out, if you ask me."

Crawley stepped around the corpse in the chair and pointed to the destroyed transmitter. "You think he was talking to the big boss on this thing?"

"That would be my guess. Probably told them Hazzard was on the case."

A somber expression masked Crawley's face. "That's exactly what I was thinking."

The newshound jotted a few lines in his notebook and then excused himself. He told the inspector he wanted to file his story for the early afternoon edition. The ambulances were screaming down the block as Crawley exited the apartment building. Walking around the corner to the alley, he saw another handful of officers in the now opened garage. They were all clustered around the gray sedan with the tripod on its roof.

Crawley made a mental note to leave word with Chambers that the auto, this one undamaged, should be delivered to Hazzard Labs as soon as possible. There, Wash MacGowan's team could continue their inspection of the sophisticated device.

As the first of three white ambulances pulled up to the curb in front of the building, the reporter moved further into the alleyway. With so much noise and activity, no one gave him any notice as he leaned back against the side of the building and closed his eyes. The warmth of the sun bathed his face as he calmed his breathing and began the mental exercises Captain Hazzard had taught all his assistants. Crawley had never attempted to contact Hazzard over such a tremendous distance before. Still, the basic tenets of telepathy allowed for the ability to cross immeasurable space, provided the parties involved were adept at the process.

Now all those hours spent under Hazzard's careful tutoring were about to be sorely tested. His mind at complete ease, the veteran newshound began to send out his thoughts into the ether.

Captain Hazzard...he thought precisely, seeing his leader's face n his mind's eye...Captain Hazzard...hear me!

Calling Captain Hazzard...danger ahead!

CHAPTER SEVEN

Sky Sharks Again

It was somewhere over Mexico that the temperature reached the danger line, and Tyler Randall stopped the rocket motor. The sudden decrease in speed was apparent instantly, though the *Silver Bullet* was doing two-hundred-eighty miles an hour. The rocket motor would have to cool for at least an hour before it could be restarted.

Randall eased back in his seat, watching the vast country terrain whiz by below. Captain Hazzard dozed in the pilot's chair, his head back against the padded rest. Although it appeared to the public at large that he was virtually a superman, Kevin Douglas Hazzard was really only human – albeit a superb example of such – and still required the basic things all people need to sustain themselves, including sleep to recharge one's physical stamina. Long ago, in the monasteries of Tibet, Hazzard had been taught the tricks of total relaxation – the ability to go into deep REM (rapid eye movement) sleep instantly and then to awaken completely refreshed and revitalized. Such was the case now, as his chest barely moved with his easy, shallow breathing.

In the rear compartments, both Wash MacGowen and Jake Cole were also availing themselves of the quiet time to catch some shut-eye. Whereas Martin Tracey and Mary Parker were very much alert, having carried on a lively conversation to assay the girl's insatiable curiosity in regards to Hazzard and his team.

When she learned that Tracey was in fact a registered surgeon, with a resume that included internship at some of the finest hospitals in the country, she was completely taken aback.

"But you're are a doctor," she said, wide-eyed. "You should be sitting in some fancy office somewhere, seeing patients and building a practice. How on earth did you come to be here, with Captain Hazzard, traipsing all over the globe on fantastic adventures?"

The good looking M.D. grinned boyishly, a trait Mary Parker found nearly irresistible. That the good doctor was a lady's man was quite apparent. Still, he seemed genuinely sincere and she listened to his words with rapt attention.

"Oh, it's not really all that big a mystery, Mary. You see, Capt... Kevin is my first cousin."

The girl's wide stare returned. "He is?!"

"Yes. After the terrible explosion that killed his parents and blinded Kevin, he came to live with us in Boston. You see, our mothers were sisters. My parents became his legal guardians, and except for the times he was away at the school for the blind, Kevin was brought up in our home.

"I was still a toddler when he arrived, and I guess I just grew up thinking of him as an older brother. There isn't anything I wouldn't do for him. By the time he reached college age, Kevin had regained his sight and devoted his life to the betterment of mankind. He went to earn degrees in all the sciences."

"And you went into medicine," Mary Parker chimed in, fascinated by the entire tale.

"Oh, yes. It wasn't a hard choice. You see, my father is a doctor. It's all I ever wanted to be. Still, after I finished my studies and internship, I began to realize that a normal life, even as a surgeon, would pale in comparison to the mission Kevin had taken upon himself. When he began constructing Hazzard Labs from the monies his parents had left him and my father had invested over the years, I approached him and offered my services to his noble undertaking. We've been together ever since."

"That's an wonderful story," Mary Parker said. "I think Captain

Hazzard is very fortunate to such a faithful friend...and brother."

In the cockpit, the subject of their discussion was hearing a familiar voice in his dreams. A voice that signaled danger.

Captain Hazzard...danger ahead!

He eyes opened and he sat up instantly alert.

And as though the malign intelligence of the Phoenix had timed it perfectly, his agents chose that time to strike again. Terror reached out of the skies at Hazzard's party, terror that made even Hazzard feel fear.

As the hot sun came over the mountains of Mexico like a silver, ghostly circle, two biplanes rose swiftly in the sky from a hidden base to meet the *Silver Bullet*. They were two identical planes flying three hundred yards apart, holding their course steadily like ships in army formation.

"What is it, Captain?" Randall queried, as his chief took over the controls. For an answer, Hazzard indicated the sky to their starboard, from whence the two aircraft were approaching. "Trouble?"

"I don't know yet," came the reply. Hazzard's impressions of a mental alert from William Crawley were vague, elusive now that he was fully awake. Had it just been a dream? There also existed the possibility that the two newcomers were government ships, planes patrolling in connection with the Mexican Rurales.

But when he changed his course a little and climbed higher, the planes ahead changed, too. Not only that, they seemed to be hedging to get the *Silver Bullet* between them.

Then Captain Hazzard's sharp eye saw something that brought him up taut with dread. On top of one ship, dimly outlined against the glare of the sun, was a spidery web of rods and wires – one of the strange tungsten-barium aerials of the Curtain of Death.

Hazzard pressed a button that sounded a gong in the main cabins behind the cockpit. Everyone on board, save Mary Parker, understood that the sound of the gong meant deadly danger. MacGowan and Jake Cole came awake fast, whereas Tracey informed the girl as to the significance of the alarm.

In the cockpit, Hazzard snapped orders. "Man the machine gun, Randall." Over the intercom he directed the orders. "Martin, look out for Miss Parker. See that her seatbelt is fastened. Jake, get in the turret with your rifle. We're going to need it. Wash, you're about to witness the Death Curtain in action!"

Hazzard side-slipped and veered. Wind shrieked in the wings of the *Silver Bullet*. One of the strange death-curtain planes dropped formation suddenly and dived to the right. The maneuver almost got Hazzard between them. Across the sky, like a faint and horrible aura, stretched a spotty curtain of fire. The shimmering, uncanny beams spread out, touched, retreated and touched again.

Wash MacGowen's nose was practically flattened against the window portal in the rear cabin, taking in the electric light show. He understood the immediate threat the shimmering veil posed to them, but as a scientist, he could not help but be mesmerized by what he was seeing.

Hazzard had no such luxury. There was sweat on his forehead. The nose of the *Silver Bullet* was almost aimed straight at the death light. It seemed that nothing could stop them from diving through it. Hazzard knew the horrible end that faced them if they did. The image of John Roan's corpse was still fresh in his memory.

He shoved the throttle to the quadrant stop. He pulled the stick back into his lap and brought the plane's nose up in a hurtling, roaring zoom. The *Bullet* climbed like a demon as though terror had even struck at its steel heart. Up till it was hanging on its propellers, up still farther till it was on its back. And, as it made a mighty zoom, its tail surface brushed that cloud of weird light.

Hazzard felt again that fearful dizziness that had come when he was standing at the top of Mary Parker's steps. He flipped the *Silver Bullet* over in an Immelmann turn, knowing that he had saved himself and his party only by a few spare feet. He was roaring in the opposite direction now; he had lost speed in the zoom. The other ships, using their quicker maneuverability, headed him off. The light curtain swept toward them again.

This time Hazzard waited, while the nearest of the hostile planes bored in. He seemed to be inviting the death they held out to him. He let his ship stall, drop off like a falling leaf – as though it were out of control.

"One of the strange death-curtain planes dropped formation
suddenly dived to the right. The manuever almost got Hazzard
between them. Across the sky, like a faint and horrible aura,
stretched a spotty curtain of fire."

Then suddenly, with the weird light almost upon them, Hazzard brought the *Silver Bullet* back under control. He flattened her out, side-slipped directly toward the nearest of the two approaching ships.

He heard the crack of Jake Cole's rifle. Looking back, he caught a glimpse of the hatless cowboy standing in the open turret. Leather straps kept Cole from falling out of the craft.

Thus the lanky cowboy was shooting with the nonchalance of a rodeo performer. He was actually chewing gum. His jaw worked rhythmically. *Crack! Crack!* His rifle spoke twice more. Hot shell casings leaped out of the ejector as though in savage glee.

"*Yeehaw!*" He exclaimed loudly. "I got'em!"

The nearest plane with the tripod on it suddenly canted its wings and fell away. The light curtain sank down after it, a bizarre mesh drawn by those spider-web rods. The sky ahead of the *Silver Bullet* was clear. Then the curtain vanished entirely as the mechanism in the strange plane ceased to function. The plane swooped earthward in a long, erratic dive.

They watched it go down; saw sunlight reflect off its wings, saw it fall straight toward the rocky side of a mountain. Then suddenly, a red rose seemed to blossom on the cliffs. The rose was followed by black smoke and the plane disappeared. During the crash, the second plane had fled.

Wash assisted Cole in getting out of his harness as he dropped down out of the open turret.

"Well done, Jake. You just saved all our lives."

"Me and Miss Betsy," he held up the high-powered Remington, "were glad to oblige." His wheat colored hair was a mess and he smoothed it down as best he could with his free. Wash tapped a button and a steel plate closed the round opening, at the same time shutting out the cold draft.

Martin Tracey handed the cowboy his hat as he moved back into the cabin. "Great shooting, Jake!"

"Thanks, Doc." Cole put his big Stetson on and grinned. "Did I ever tell you, Miss Betsy was a gift from Buffalo Bill Cody?"

Tracey made a sour face. "Yes, you did. Many, many times."

Mary Parker slapped Tracey's arm. "Oh, but I haven't heard it. Did you really meet the famous Buffalo Bill, Mister Cole?"

"Indeed I did, ma'am. And please call me Jake."

As Cole sat down across from the girl and began his narrative, Tracey and MacGowen both smiled and resigned themselves to hearing Cole's tall tale for the hundredth time.

They reached Guatemala three hours later, and the great volcanic peaks of San Pedro, Santa Maria and Toliman lifted up on the horizon. The *Silver Bullet* sped over green jungles, high mountain ridges dotted with Indian villages and shimmering clear blue lakes. Hazzard decided to fly to the compass point John Roan had mentioned in his note before trying to land.

Tracey explained to Mary Parker that they were close to their goal now. She came forward into the cockpit to find Captain Hazzard studying his compass. Randall was flying the plane while Hazzard had a map of Guatemala in front of him painted on a transparent membrane, set in a boxlike frame.

Thin lines of light from mirrors underneath showed on the map. They moved slowly. Where they crossed was the current position of the plane.

It was another of Hazzard's inventions, his tele-autographic compass. He had many such transparent maps of all sections of the globe. By fitting them into the frame he could see his exact location in relation to topographical points.

The lines were converging now at north latitude 13, west longitude 89. Mary Parker's cheeks flushed as the plane sped forward, and the lines crawled ever closer to the Espiritu Santo range.

The mountains were under their nose now, high, volcanic, rugged. They crossed the main ridge, swept over a deep basin of dense jungle stretching for several miles. Another peak rose in its center, conical and grim. The plane bored on. The cone-shaped mountain had a feather of smoke stuck in a crater at its top. It came steadily nearer. They were close to it now-passing over it. The lines of the map showed 15.10-10-89-27.

"Now!" Captain Hazzard pointed. Mary Parker shook her head in sudden dismay as she looked out the window past his shoulder.

"That? It can't be! It's a volcano. There's nothing on it. No one could live down there!"

CHAPTER EIGHT

Green Fury

Captain Hazzard, too, stared tensely at that forbidding peak. Tumbled cliffs. Barren slopes. Deserted ravines. Not a vestige of grass. The green wall of the jungle halted at the edge of the volcanic rock as if eruptions in the past had put a dreadful curse on all growing things.

"How...how shall we find him?" Mary Parker's face showed that she had already lost faith in the search for her father.

But Captain Hazzard said nothing. He kicked the rudder, thrust the stick sidewise, brought the *Silver Bullet* around in a steep-banked turn. In the descending spirals, he lost altitude. The black, sinister crater of the mountain rose to meet them.

He passed directly over it. Heat from those subterranean depths made bumpy air. The *Silver Bullet* rocked and bucked. He circled then, skirted the outer ridges of the crater.

"Dead as the moon, Captain," commented Tyler Randall.

The rest of the team had all crowded in behind Mary Parker and one by one they added their own observations.

From Jake Cole, grimly: "I'll be a horned toad if even a gopher could pitch tent down there!"

Martin Tracey nodded. "Those figures Roan wrote in that message must be off, Cap. Maybe the ant bites made him nutty."

"And yet," Wash MacGowen said, stroking his long chin judicially, "doesn't it seem a little strange that those numbers should exactly correspond to this peak? It is the only mountain in this immediate jungle area. More than coincidence, I should say."

Hazzard was thinking the same thing. Though nothing showed on that grim mountain, he wasn't satisfied that John Roan's figures were wrong. From the first, the Phoenix had been clothed in mystery. The mere fact of their recent encounter with the two enemy biplanes was evidence enough that the criminal mastermind had his base somewhere in this general vicinity.

Mary Parker repeated her question. "How can we find my father?"

Hazzard turned to her. "There's only one way. Investigate that volcano."

"But there's no place to land, even if –"

"No." Hazzard looked at his map. "Lake Izabal is forty miles away. The nearest landing field is fifty. But there's an Indian village ten miles back. I saw it when we came over. You and Randall will go on to the airstrip, while the rest of us will drop in there via parachutes."

"Then we can reach the mountain hiking through the jungle."

"The rest of us!" The girl repeated the words and a look of consternation crossed her lovely face. "You mean you won't take me? That's not fair! Not after I've come this far with you."

"Mary, have you ever made a parachute jump?" asked Hazzard, hoping to discourage her.

"No. But surely you can show me what to do! Anything – and I do mean anything – to be with you when you find my father. Please, Captain, you can't refuse me now." There was no fear in her eyes. Hazzard still had his doubts, but reluctantly he came around. There was no denying that Mary Parker had the right stuff in her.

"All right, you win," he conceded. "I'll let you use a special 'chute we have, one with a self-operating ripcord. You jump...it does the rest."

He headed the nose north, swept over ten miles of jade green jungle and saw the Indian village again. The architecture told him it belonged to a tribe of Chicastenangos.

They came running out to the streets as the plane swept low. They had queer costumes of bright red and blue. The men wore big-brimmed hats. The women had on halos, twenty-foot strips of red-and-blue hand-woven cloth wrapped around their copper-colored bodies. Their hair was black as night. The village was a tiny cluster of adobe houses perched on a terraced hillock that rose out of the jungle. There was a small square in it.

Hazzard noted the wind directions. If they bailed out at just the right altitude from just the right position, the wind drift would carry them into the village. He turned the controls over to Randall who could be depended upon to jockey them exactly into the right drop position.

Wash went first. All of Hazzard's men had made parachute jumps before. Wash made the drop as unemotionally as he'd add a column of figures. Jumping out of a plane into an exotic jungle locale was all in a day's work when one worked for Captain Hazzard. There was a special trapdoor in the *Silver Bullet's* floor. Wash simply climbed into his 'chute harness, secured it and then fell through. Jake followed, chewing a new wad of gum as he tied his Stetson's side strings tightly under his chin so as not to lose his favorite hat on his way down. He blew out a pink balloon through his lips and then popped it back into his mouth laughingly. Jake claimed that chewing helped him count off the seconds before he pulled the ripcord.

The cowboy leaped into space with a loud, "Geronimo!"

Hazzard dropped the parachutes of equipment next. Wash and Jake would be on the ground before they landed, so that the Indians wouldn't appropriate them.

Then Tracey jumped, looking anxiously at Mary Parker as he did so. He'd already come to feel a proprietary interest in the girl. But Captain Hazzard put her into the auto-ripcord parachute himself. As team leader, he was not one to relegate anything that involved the safety of innocent civilians. There was a small, clock-like device on the back of the harness which could be set to jerk the ripcord at any given moment. Hazzard set it carefully and led the nervous girl to the now closed trap panels. Her face was pale, but she was smiling. She looked voluptuous and athletic in her tropical shorts.

Hazzard strapped an automatic and a hunting knife around her waist, tied a first-aid kit containing anti-venom for snake bites and a water canteen on it. As he adjusted the leather belt, he was all too conscious of her nearness and the ever-present scent of roses.

Her chest rose and fell with her anxiety.

"Just relax and breathe normally," he suggested.

"Easier said than done," she replied, blowing out a puff of air and making an effort to calm her nerves. "I'm all set. Really. What next?"

"After the 'chute opens," he explained, "just pull the shroud lines in the direction you want to go. Spill a little air out and you can steer the thing like a glider. Do you understand?"

"Yes, I think I do."

"Good. Are you ready?"

She nodded and stepped to the trap.

Hazzard pressed a button and Mary Parker dropped into space. He watched to see her 'chute open, then got ready to jump himself. "We'll keep in touch with you by radio," he said to Randall over the comm link. "You can let us know when you reach that airstrip."

In the cockpit, Randall grinned. Taking care of the *Silver Bullet* was his special pride. "Roger that, Captain. Good hunting."

Hazzard stepped easily through the trap and plunged into space. He didn't pull the cord till the ground was a few hundred feet below. The delayed silk deployment enabled him to catch up with the others. He touched down at the same time Wash and Jake did, and he was able to help Mary Parker gather up the folds of 'chute when she landed close to the little square. She was radiantly beaming with obvious pride at having made her first successful jump.

But there was no time for congratulations.

Indians swarmed around them, staring curiously. Some made signs to ward off evil spirits. Others grinned, showing ivory teeth. Most of the Indians in Guatemala were friendly. Naked, copper-colored kids ran up and poked at their chutes and equipment till Wash shooed them away.

Hazzard was an expert linguist ,and he addressed the Chicasten-angos in their native language. "Quichi lana," he said, pointing to the cone of the volcano ten miles away. "Un nihongi atlan...I go through jungle. Tulul cuintla pan zumala...we need a guide."

A change came over the Indians. Their faces sobered. Many backed away. Others shook their heads. "Chal! Chal!...No!" they cried. "Huetenzo!...Accursed!"

There was fear in their eyes and they began to talk vehemently. They told Hazzard that people from their village never went to the mountain now. A few had in the past and never came back. No trace of them had ever been found. The mountain was Huetenzo, cursed in some strange way. It's name was Omoxotl, which meant "Terror's Shadow."

Besides that, there were murderous Indians in the jungle, fierce Tzutuhiles left over from the tribes that even Cortez's lieutenant, Don Alvarado, had been unable to subdue. There were poisonous snakes and dangerous animals.

Hazzard glimpsed one Indian at the edge of the crowd who didn't seem as excited as the others at the talk of going into the jungle. He wore a spray of the rare figa-figa berries in his hat, which meant that he understood jungle magic. And in his belt was the fang of the giant snake, which meant he was a great hunter.

"Your name?" asked Hazzard, pointing suddenly.

"Ulzi," said the Indian promptly.

"You are a mighty hunter," declared Hazzard. "You know the jungle trails. You are a great witch-doctor. The evil spirits cannot scare you. You will lead the people-who-dropped-from-the-sky to Omoxotl."

Still the Indian looked doubtful, and there was a glint of fear in his eyes. Hazzard continued: "I, too, am a great witch-doctor....Watch!"

He always carried a kit of chemicals in his knapsack. These, along with the gadgets in his utility belt, made a wide range of chemical "magic" possible. He brought two small empty test tubes out now and a piece of white cloth that had been dipped in cobalt-chloride. Ulzi nodded, grunted skeptically.

Hazzard slipped a lump of calcium in one tube and held his finger over it. This absorbed moisture, making the air inside the test tube dry. He drew his thumb away quickly, put the white cloth in, then again covered the top of the test tube.

"Look!"

Before Ulzi's startled eyes, the white cloth turned a vivid blue. The Indians watching exclaimed in admiration. Ulzi looked awestruck, then quickly hardened face into a mask to show that hew as not impressed.

Hazzard took another strip of the white, cobalt-chloride-treated cloth and placed it in the second test tube along with a drop of water to make the air damp. This strip turned a vivid pink. Ulzi couldn't prevent his eyes from growing wide with wonder.

Then Hazzard took a small nickel-plated flashlight from his pocket and gave it to the Indian. "For the great hunter and magician," he said, "who will lead the white witch-doctor and his friends through the jungle to Omoxotl!"

Ulzi nodded and struck his chest, his pride aroused by Hazzard's flattery and his competitive spirit by Hazzard's trick. "Ulzi's own magic is so great he does not fear Omoxotl," he said.

Hazzard picked up his knapsack and pointed toward the forest. The other members of his party gathered their things. Following Ulzi, they started down the terraced hill toward the green wall of the jungle. The Indians watched them go, shaking their heads and muttering. Just as they reached the jungle, the Chicastenangos began a chant – low, wailing, monotonous, rising and falling in a minor cadence.

"What are they singing?" Mary Parker inquired, taking her place behind Captain Hazzard and in front of Martin Tracey in the procession. Hazzard looked to Ulzi who was walking ahead of him and translated the girl's questions. Ulzi waved his hands towards the massive tropical forest before them and uttered several short sentences in his native tongue.

Hazzard looked over his shoulder at the others, the singing in the distance getting louder. "It is the chant for great hunters doomed not to return from the never-never land."

Mary gulped. Jake Cole removed his big Stetson and waved it at the singing villagers. "So long, amigos. Thanks for the cheery send-off."

With that, the small, bronze man led the five adventurers into the dark, steamy, lush world before them.

The Guatemalan jungle grew ominously still after they had been walking for two hours. The group had trekked along, walking amongst the tall hardwoods and cutting a path through the overhanging vines and creepers. The humid air was cloying and all of them were sweating, as their boots clumped along the spongy, moss-covered ground. Up until now, myriad shafts of golden light penetrating the canopy high above had buoyed their spirits along with the many sounds of animal wildlife all around them. The abrupt cessation of all noise was unnatural and gave both Ulzi and Captain Hazzard pause. Even the ever annoying monkeys had stopped chattering and the dozens of bright-colored birds visible only seconds earlier, were suddenly gone.

Ulzi rolled his eyes nervously and stopped in the middle of a small clearing. Hazzard felt the first vibrations of a psychic warning that danger was creeping close.

The eerie stillness of the jungle wrapped itself around them like a brooding, malevolent thing.

"What is it?" Mary Parker spoke up. "What's happening?"

Martin Tracey touched her elbow and brought his index finger to his lips to caution her to remain quiet.

It seemed suddenly to Hazzard that eyes were watching them... hostile eyes, baleful and murderous.

Hazzard's gaze darted upward suddenly. He saw the rustle of giant leaves in the great Ceiba tree ahead of them, under which the trail wound.

"Look out!" His warning was not soon enough. Something streaked down like a flash of light from its green branches.

It struck Ulzi in the chest, and the copper-hued hunter fell with a piercing cry. Mary, hand to her mouth, screamed as Ulzi lay on his back with a green-plumed spear sticking out of his chest.

Hazzard's arm was a blur as he drew his .45 automatic, aimed and fired at almost the same time. There was another cry from the Ceiba's dense branches. The foliage moved, rustled and a body hurled from it and fell beside Ulzi at the edge of the trail. High above, black vultures appeared, their wings flapping greedily.

Captain Hazzard and the others ran forward. The man who had speared Ulzi lay on his back with his eyes wide open, glaring. There was a hole drilled through his head. It was no wonder Hazzard hadn't seen him until too late. The dead man wore a green cloak of quetzal feathers, brilliant as the foliage. His face was the color of the reddish tree branches. It was perfect camouflage. The only conspicuous thing about him was the metal headband that held a bright, gleaming jewel in the center of his forehead.

Mary Parker was on the ground beside Ulzi, tenderly holding his head up against her legs. He let out a moan. "Chlan cuinali," he rasped in pain.

"What does he mean?" asked Wash somberly. The team was gathered around their fallen guide.

"The Jewel Men," said Hazzard. "They are Tzutuhiles...the worst Indians going. But..." Crouching down opposite the girl, his hand reached out and touched the spear in the native's body. Ulzi lay still, his head tilted to the side in eternal repose. Mary Parker gently laid it on the soft ground. Hazzard's eyes were bright with consternation. With reverence, he took hold of the lethal lance and yanked it free. Rising to his feet, he examined it. "This spear has a metal shaft... made of hollow tubing like a golf club."

"What!" Wash took hold of the spear and then passed it to Jake and Tracey.

"Well, don't that beat all," Cole whistled around his chewing gum. "What's it mean, Captain?"

"It means, Jake, that some white man has armed them recently... some white man who is using them as guards to keep everyone else away."

"The Phoenix!" Mary Parker deduced, getting to her with feet with Tracey's help.

"Exactly." Even as Hazzard spoke, something whispered through the branches. If he hadn't ducked instantly a green-plumed spear would have stretched him beside Ulzi.

"Run!" Hazzard pointed toward some black rock formations where huge vultures were perched. In the clearing, they were exposed and vulnerable. Sinister as the rocks and their sentinels looked, they offered the only place of refuge.

CHAPTER NINE

Slaves of Fire

The air was filled suddenly with steel-shafted spears, whistling, hissing, thudding. One came so close to Hazzard's face he could feel the breeze of it. Another zipped past his back. Hazzard opened fire with his automatic.

Martin, Jake and Wash began shooting. Tracey held onto Mary Parker's with his free hand, while plugging away at the surrounding brush. Cordite fumes drifted through the leaves. The crack of their weapons made a steady tattoo as they ran for the rocks.

Another Indian toppled out of a high Ceiba tree where he'd been hiding. He did a somersault in the air, landed on a lower limb and hung there gruesome for a moment, blood dripping from his neck.

A savage fifty-to-one side came charging out of a bush and Hazzard fired from the hip. The gaudy attacker took three steps forward with a bullet in his heart, then dropped. Jake, who had taken up the rear guard position, was taking a steady toll with his high-powered rifle. He shot as fast as he could slide the bolt action and pump the trigger. He never missed once, effectively decimating the enemy ranks. But the whole jungle seemed filled with savages. Bullets alone would never let Hazzard's party reach the rocks.

Hazzard tugged desperately at his belt and drew out another of his unique smoke bombs. This one gave off a whit vapor that Hazzard used in conjunction with a pair of infrared goggles. He hurriedly slipped the goggles on now, wishing he'd brought enough for the whole team. But he hadn't. The lives of all of them depended on this single pair.

He pulled the striker of the bomb, tossed it tensely and heard it explode with a violent pouff. White smoke spurted. It was soon denser than fog. It slipped through the leaves in ghostly streamers, crept along the ground.

Hazzard heard the Tzutuhiles yelling. The infrared ray goggles picked up light waves on one end of the spectrum only – the end which the white smoke did not touch – enabling him to see dimly through the vapor which blinded all the others.*

----

*AUTHOR'S NOTE - ***

Captain Hazzard got his idea for these when army aerial photographers recently took pictures of New York City through a bank of dense clouds. They used an infrared ray filter on their lens. They couldn't see the ground, but the camera films were affected by the infrared rays coming up through the clouds.

Martin, Wash, Jake and Mary Parker were already turned around, groping helplessly. Hazzard ran up to them, made them hold hands, and put himself at the head of the chain. He told Jake, whose ears were very sharp, to follow the sound of his footsteps.

Strung out in this fashion, Hazzard led his party toward the rocks. But the Tzutuhiles hadn't been scared off yet. They were fierce, murderous warriors eager for the kill. Hazzard saw one of them directly in his path. The Tzutuhile couldn't see him, but the Indian's ears, as sensitive as Jake's, had detected the sound of their steps.

The Jewel Man suddenly gave out a cry that told his fellow tribesmen that he had located the prey. It was like the cry of a killer wolf calling his slavering pack. He raised his spear to fling it the direction of Hazzard's footsteps.

Hazzard dodged when the spear came whistling past his head. Then he ran forward toward the Tzutuhile. The man shrieked again and stood his ground, eyes smarting in the thick smoke, lips curling away from hideous teeth that had been filed to points. Squinting, he tried to peer through the smoke. He pulled out a long, sharp knife and lunged straight at Hazzard.

Still Hazzard didn't shoot. That would have meant giving away their exact position. Instead, he crouched on one knee quickly, seized the knife wrist of the leaping savage, and used the Indian's own momentum to lift him and hurl him through the air.

The green-robed Indian whirled over Hazzard's head and struck the ground with a thud. The knife flew out of his hand on impact. Angrily, he bounced up and came back at Captain Hazzard. Hazzard felled him this time with a hard blow to the forehead from his gun butt. The Indian pitched forward, senseless.

The rocks were directly ahead now. The vultures were lighting up on broad wings as the smoke rolled towards them.

Their furious croaks mingled with the war screams of the Tzutuhiles.

Three of the Jewel Men came together and seemed to agree on some strategem. Holding their steel-shafted-spears in line they ran straight at Hazzard's group.

Hazzard knew then that the smoke was thinning, that the Indians could see. He yanked his goggles aside and made sure of it. The Tzutuhiles' arms were drawing back. Another instant and at least on of Hazzard's team would be struck by knife-sharp steel.

"Drop!"

Jake Cole and the others obeyed Hazzard's order as two of the spears came flying over their heads. The crack of Hazzard's .45 broke the arm of the third Indian. The two others came on with their knives. Hazzard fired twice more and the Tzutuhiles fell back in alarm nursing broken fingers. Hazzard had shot the blades right out of their hands.

But there was no time to lose. The smoke was vanishing rapidly and with it their only advantage. From all around, the Jewel Men were closing in.

Captain Hazzard mounted the rocks and then helped Jake Cole after him. Jake pulled the rest of the party. The first fringe of volcanic boulders ended sharply. Behind them was another higher group, pitted with potholes and caves. Some gigantic upheaval of nature thousands of years before had left these weird monuments. There were natural bridges, caverns, huge upthrust spires.

Hazzard found a great, high-roofed cavern that had only two places to enter and here they stopped. From here they could effectively stand off the Tzutuhiles. Hazzard folded his goggles and put them away. At the same time he took a quick inventory of the arsenal in his utility belt. If their bullets failed, he still had plenty of tear-gas pellets.

The green-garbed Indians appeared on the outer wall. But slugs from Jake's rifle made them hesitate to come closer. Every time a jeweled forehead showed itself, Jake made powdered rock spurt in the Indian's face.

When the Indians showed no sign of making a rush, Hazzard stationed Jake at one entrance, Martin at the other. Then he announced:

"When it gets dark, I'm going to visit Omoxotl. The four of you will stay here till I get back. That should be in five or six hours. You've got the portable radio. If I don't show up by daybreak, call Randall. Get him to use the high-powered radio in the plane to get in touch with the government of Guatemala. They'll send soldiers to rescue you."

Mary Parker's dark eyes were filled with apprehension. "But the Indians will kill you! They're waiting in the jungle. How will you get through?"

"Don't worry about that, ma'am," said Jake Cole grimly. "The Captain could slip in an Indian's ear and the varmint would never know it. But..." he looked at Hazzard pleadingly, "...you'll be needing company. You'd better take me with you, just to be sure."

"Sorry, Jake, I can't. Miss Parker has to be guarded. The Tzutuhiles might get it into their heads to attack in the dark. As it is, we've got to roll rocks up to both entrances. We'd best get to it."

They spent the afternoon making the cave safe against an all-out assault. Hazzard was sure that Jake and the others would be able to hold it unless something utterly unforeseen happened. But he wasn't so sure that he could get back. Visiting Omoxotl at night was like a challenge hurled in the teeth of Fate.

Yet, when the night came, he slipped out quietly. The tropic blackness swallowed him. The trees seemed to enfold him in their branches. Those long years when he had been blind himself, living in darkness, had borne strange fruit. His muscles were trained like an animal's to act on instant reflexes. He had learned to walk swiftly, warily on springy toes. His clairvoyance made him aware of things that the physical eye couldn't see.

He passed across the outer wall of rocks until a musky smell in the air told him that a lurking Tzutuhile was close at hand. The feeling of danger, the mysterious telepathic vibration that a hostile mind gave out, made it possible for him to avoid the savage. He moved on quickly, stealthily into the solemn terror that was the jungle at night.

Hazzard heard a death scream of some small animal struck down, proof that most of the wilderness' fiercest predators were nocturnal. He heard the horrid bubbling smacks of a jaguar feasting on fresh-killed meat. Once his senses screamed a different warning. The inner realms of his mind whispered: "Snake!"

A muskiness quite different from that of the Indian odor reached his nostrils. It was pungent, sickening. A reptilian odor this time. He crouched back behind a tree and waited while a great, forty-foot anaconda writhed its terrible crushing coils across the jungle floor.

Then Hazzard caught the smell of a man again. He crouched and waited. The shuffle of bare feet sounded soon. That meant he was near a trail. And as he crouched, one of the Jewel Men went by, walking in the direction of Omoxotl.

Moving silently, running from tree to tree like a specter, Hazzard followed him mile after mile. All the while his sense of direction told him that they were getting nearer the mountain.

He was sure of it when the ground began to rise. The sponginess left the earth. The trees began to thin. Suddenly, they ceased altogether and Hazzard was out in a world of barren rock.

The footsteps of the Indian were fainter now, more muffled. Hazzard hurried ahead till he felt a sudden warm eddy of air on his face. The air, besides being warmer, had a different smell to it, a faint odor of sulphur. Hazzard surmised that he was standing close to a passage through the rocks.

He moved in and heard the feet of the Indian just ahead of him. The man muttered something, and another guttural voice replied. A guard! Hazzard crept forward as stealthily as a night cat. When the Indian he'd been following went on, Hazzard sprang at the guard, ducking the spear that was thrust toward him. Hazzard stilled the cry of the guard's lips by a smashing punch to the jaw. The guard collapsed unconscious and Hazzard lowered his limp body and sped after the Indian who was his unknowing guide.

The passage went up now. It seemed to go interminably through the very heart of the rock. An endless corridor of stifling, sulphurous darkness.

Then Hazzard glimpsed a faint glow ahead of him, reflected on the smooth sides of the passage, making it possible for him to get a dim silhouette of the man in front. He stopped a moment later, peering along another passage that ran off sharply to the right. There was a great room with a domed ceiling – a natural cavern in the mountain with great, high stone-buttressed walls.

But it wasn't the chamber that caught his quick interest. It was the men in it. Chained men, toiling at some unknown task before gleaming holes in the rock.

The sulphur smell was stronger now. A faint acrid haze hung in the air. Out of those furnace-like pits came glowing light. The men's bodies were bathed in sweat. He could see the glisten of it. He wasn't close enough to see their faces to know whether Mary Parker's father and his partner, Kurt Gordon, were among them.

He couldn't even tell whether these were white men. Their skins were blackened, burned. But they were slaves obviously, chained to some grueling work, held against their will before those weird holes of fire. And Hazzard realized in a flash that the Phoenix was using the power of the great volcano, Omoxotl, for some strange purpose of his own.

He crept closer, trying to get a better look at the men. He noted then there that were other bizarre figures in the room who were not chained – Indians dressed in hideous costumes made from the skins of anacondas, with the gaping heads of the great serpents serving as parka-like hoods. The fangs had been left in. The eyes had been ornamented with green jewels. Python Men!

And they had whips, long scourges of plaited leather. As he watched, a whip flashed out with a crack like a pistol shot. It flayed the naked shoulders of a chained slave who had dared to pause in whatever he was doing. The slave gave choking scream of pain and stumbled back to his work.

Hazzard's nerves were taut. This was like some nightmare, like a world of fantastic horror such as a madman might conceive.

As much as he itched to help the poor souls trapped by the merciless Python Men, he was but one man. Reckless bravado on his part would only lead to defeat now. He tried to see more. His curiosity spurred him on. Even that boldness nearly brought him to disaster. For a sudden whisper of sound in the darkness behind him made him turn. He was almost too late.

Three silent Python Men, dressed in snakeskins, had crept upon him. He could see the gleam of their coal-black eyes, the shine of their cruel faces. They had whips, too. They were evidently guards who had come to relieve the others in the big chamber watching over the slaves.

Hazzard leaped straight at them...a thing they didn't expect. They lifted the heavy butts of their whips, tried to rain stunning blows on his head. Moving like greased lightning, he avoided all their strikes. Then he snatched one whip away, cracked a man with its butt, then grabbed him as he fell and swung him violently, knocking the others down like bowling pins. He leaped between them before they could rise and grab his legs.

It would be fatal to everything if he were caught by them now.

He ran into a side corridor that slanted off darkly to the right. The Python Men were following, and he knew by their cries and the sounds of other footsteps that the guards in the work room had joined them in pursuit.

They chased him for perhaps five minutes, then stopped abruptly. Hazzard stopped, too, listening, wondering why they'd seemingly given up trying to apprehend him. There was no sound now. The silence was eerie, forbidding, and Hazzard's scalp prickled with an intimation that something was wrong. His hand slipped to one of the pouches on his belt and in a second he clicked on his flashlight.

For a moment he saw nothing out of the ordinary. He was standing in a rock-walled passage. It had an uneven ceiling pitted with many holes. It sloped ahead of him on a gentle grade. Then Hazzard noticed a black vent close to the floor of the corridor about ten feet away, and two more farther on.

And as he looked, something came through them...wisps of yellow, writing, sulphurous smoke. The smoke became red suddenly, red with glowing flame.

Using the beam of his flashlight, Hazzard moved toward it, eyes wide with wonder. The flame broadened. The glowing smoke had substance to it now. It was thick, bubbling, oozing forward steadily out of the vents. It hissed on the floor, spread out like pancake batter. It was molten lava, he realized, poured purposely into the passage through those vents to head him off.

He took two steps forward, stopped as the hideous, bubbling pool swept toward him like an evil tide. A fiery arm of the stuff reached out like a tentacle to clutch him. Hazzard could go no farther. Behind him the Python Men waited, whips ready to shred his skin to pieces. Ahead was the quickly rising pool of burning lava.

He was trapped!

"Trapped!"

CHAPTER TEN

The Whispering Scourge

Back in the cave, Jake, Martin, Wash and Mary Parker were filled with unreasoning dread. Hours had passed. No sight or sound of Captain Hazzard had come. At the center of their makeshift base, Wash had lit a small candle to provide them with some light. They kept far away from either entrance, so as not to show their positions to the Indians who still surrounded them.

Mary Parker got a cigarette from Martin Tracey, who was still on guard at rear entrance to the cave. She brought it back to the middle and used the candle to light it. As the first puffs of nicotine served to calm her nerves, she looked at Wash. He was busy taking a quick inventory of the contents of their knapsacks.

"Just making sure everything is where we need it," he explained when he caught her staring. "No such thing as being too prepared."

"You've known Captain Hazzard a long time, haven't you?"

"Oh, yes," the kindly scientist said. "In fact, except for Tracey, I'd say more than anyone else at Hazzard lab. You see, Cap...er...Kevin was my student when he was in college."

"It's hard to imagine him as a student," Mary Parker said, drawing in another swallow from her fag. "He seems like he was born in charge."

"Ah, a very astute observation, my dear. And you are correct. Even as a student, he made no bones about asserting himself. At first I thought he was just some egotistical young pup, wet behind the ears. But as time went on and I recognized his true genius, I came to understand his earlier frustrations had been due entirely to his unquenchable thirst for knowledge.

"He never stops wanting to know more. When he graduated and started Hazzard Labs, it was in all the papers. Soon after he called to offer me the position of head of research and development. I accepted immediately, and have never regretted the decision since."

Wash went back to his inspection of their gear, and Mary continued to pace back and forth. Her boots stirred whispering echoes that mingled with the strange sounds of the night. Those night noises bothered her. A city girl most of her life, she reacted to the jungle sounds as if they originated from alien worlds beyond her comprehension. The weird cries of the howling monkeys sounded like lost souls calling out there in the dark. And the bats! They kept slipping into the cave entrances, swooping low and staring at her out of small, malevolent eyes.

But most of all, she was frightened about her father. Now that the jet black night had fallen, now that Captain Hazzard didn't come back, all her trepidations returned. She ground out her finished cigarette and went to Martin Tracey.

"Why...why do you suppose Captain Hazzard doesn't come back?" Her arms were wrapped under her heaving bosom, she shivered at an outside breeze. Her alluring eyes were big and dark.

And Martin wasn't his usual confident self, although he tried to put on a brave face for the lovely girl he'd become attached to. "Please, you shouldn't worry, Mary. Cap has proven time and again that he's more than capable of taking care of himself against any kind of trouble."

When his eyes failed to meet hers directly, she sensed his unease immediately. "You're worried too, aren't you? Please, Martin, don't lie to me as if I were a child."

He nodded. "Alright. Yes, I am worried. Not for us, mind you...I'm thinking of Cap...Kevin. I can feel...sense that something has happened and that he's in a tough spot."

"Oh!" Mary Parker shivered again and Tracey, still holding his carbine with his right hand, wrapped his left around her shoulders for comfort. She rested her head on his chest and the sweet scent of perfume made his heart beat faster.

Martin looked to Wash, who was watching them. In the bald-headed man's eyes, he had read somber agreement to his own intuition. Something had happened to Captain Hazzard. All was clearly not well with their chief. Discordant vibrations which meant trouble were coming through the unseen ether. Even Jake Cole, who had no discernible psychic abilities, felt deep in his gut that something was awry. His strong jaws moved with melancholy slowness as he stood, rifle ready, at the front door of the cave.

Then in the troubled silence that followed, Mary Parker lifted her head up and exclaimed, "Listen! What's that noise?"

They all heard it...a new sound out there in the stygian woods, a strange, uncanny whispering that seemed to fill the whole air.

"The wind, maybe," suggested Martin. "It's been still tonight, but now I guess it's rising. Those must be rustling leaves we're hearing."

Jake Cole shook his head negatively. He was all attention suddenly. His jaws had stopped. "Can't be the wind, Doc. That noise ain't in the trees...it's coming from the ground. Put out the candle, Wash. Let's see if there's anything comin'."

Wash snuffed the candle and the cave was instantly pitch dark. They could hear Jake close to the entrance, leaning against the piled-up rocks. "Nothing to see," he muttered. "No Injuns. But that noise..."

It was louder now....as steady, persistent whisper that got on Mary Parker's nerves. "The light, please!" she gasped. "I don't like this. I'm...scared."

Wash immediately lighted the candle again; but the noise did not cease. It was louder still.

The Montana was alert before the cave opening, prowling, peering, sniffing. "It beats me," he admitted. "It sounds like something crawling. I never heard nothin' like it before...except...?"

"What? What is it, Jake? If you know, please tell us," Mary Parker urged. "It's coming closer!"

Jake didn't answer, but the sound was almost upon them now. It was in the thick grass outside the cave entrance. It was the restless, persistent movement of millions of insect feet.

"Ants! I thought so!" Jake was pointing now. Then he sprang forward and slapped at the stones that blocked the entrance, beating furiously with his big, ten-gallon stetson.

Red army ants were swarming over the rocks in an endless, scurrying stream. The cave door was blocked to prevent the Tzutuhiles from entering, but space had been left for air. Through these gaps the ants were coming. Jake's efforts were making no more impression than a straw stemming a raging tide.

The ants came on. For every dozen he crushed a hundred entered. They were the fierce red ants of the tropics, the dread carnivorous insects capable of stripping flesh from human bones.

They had glistening eyes, waving antennae, eager jaws. They poured through the holes in the barricade, slipped through chinks, wriggled underneath.

Martin and Wash began beating at them too, but the ants kept coming. A thin line of them, the boldest vanguards, started up Jake's trousers. He slapped and a half dozen of the vicious insects clamped their mandibles through the denim and into his skin. "*EEyowww!*" he yelled, feeling the tiny pincers cut into him. He brushed them away frantically and they left red marks behind them.

Then Wash ran to his supplies and drew out a brown bottle.

He uncorked it, poured liquid in a thin stream around the entrance through which the ants were marching. It was strong carbolic acid for cauterizing wounds. Its pungent smell filled the air of the cave. It lay in an oily line on the floor.

The ants drove Jake and Martin back now. Their fight centered on brushing away those which had got on their clothes.

They slapped them, dashed them to the earth before stepping over Wash's carbolic acid moat.

The ants continued advancing. The foremost of them reached the acid and paused. Others pushed from behind and crawled over them. These fell into the acid, fumed, shriveled and died. Still others fell on top of them. They died, too, their red bodies smoking, but their corpses made a bridge presently over which the rest could cross. The space behind the acid line in front of the cave doorway was filled with millions of swarming, crawling insects now. They were still pouring over the stones. They swept across the line in regiments of thousands.

"It's no use!" cried Mary Parker. "They're still coming. We can't stop them. They'll drive us out!"

Mary screamed as the ants crawled up her slim, bare legs and bit her. They made red spots on her hands as she brushed them off and stamped on them. She backed away, her long, lovely legs bleeding from many small bites. Jake ran across the cave and began clawing at the other rock wall they had so meticulously built. Wash and Martin helped him, knowing what he planned to do. The ants were driving them out into the darkness, out where the Indians waited with their deadly steel spears. And there was no help for it. "If only the Captain was here!" groaned Jake, giving voice to all their thoughts. He continued working feverishly to tear down the rock embankment.

They got the stones out and quickly grabbed their knapsacks. Running, brushing the ants from their clothes as they went, they scrambled through the cave's rear exit. Behind them, steady, persisitent as doom itself, came the sound of myriad feet.

But they knew they could outrun the insects. They didn't fear being caught when it came to mere speed. It was the inky black night itself that concerned them. And they didn't know which way to go.

There was no sound of the Indians, not the faintest sign. They ran blindly for a hundred yards across an open space until another rocky hillock loomed ahead. Throwing caution to the wind, Jake had pulled out his flashlight and aimed it along the trail before them. He knew it was a beacon for hidden savages, but the alternative was tripping over roots or even animals in the dark.

Now they eyed the cluster of rocks with renewed hope. "It's better than nothing," said Jake. "We've shaken those crawling varmints. We'll build up rocks and keep the Injuns..."

He stopped. A gasp of sheer amazement escaped his lips.

The others all yelled in alarm, too, for there was a whisper in the air above them. A streak of brown stuff fell in the beam of Jake's flashlight as it descended over them. They tried to leap away, but only Jake, a few feet from the others, managed to get free. The others couldn't escape the meshes of the woven vine net that fell upon them.

It came down swiftly, layer on layer of it, crisscrossing around their heads and shoulders, dragging them down to the ground with its weight.

Above the swish of the net they heard the shrill, triumphant cries of the Tzutuhiles ranged in the bushes on the top of the wall.

Jake, getting to his feet, played the flashlight over the entangled prison that held his companions.

"Run for it, Jake!" Wash called out, ensnared in the cumbersome blanket of vines. "Go!"

But the cowboy had waited too long. Suddenly there were Indians coming at him from every direction, their spears at ready. Jake spun about, clubbed the first two with his flashlight until it was knocked from his hand. As the beam spun into the air, Mary, Wash and Tracey tried to follow the action beyond their jungle prison.

Dozens of shadowy jungle natives leaped onto the fighting cowboy, his fist flying every which way. The sounds of smacking flesh indicating the damage he was doing the Indians. But alas, their numbers were too great and he succumbed, as they kept falling over him, pummeling him with their spear ends. And then he was mercifully knocked out.

The Tzutuhiles began jumping up and down in an impromptu victory dance over their fallen foe.

* * * *

In the heart of Omoxotl, Captain Hazzard climbed desperately through a narrow, natural chimney in the rock. It was in the roof of the passage through which he'd been running when the red-hot lava had appeared.

He had seen the fumes of sulphurous smoke draw up to this vent. He didn't know where it led. He wasn't sure he'd be able to squeeze through it. He'd climbed into it as the only alternative to being burned to death or captured by the Phoenix.

His skin was sore now, burning. He knew now what had made John Roan's face have that reptilian look. The man had obviously been chained, of course, in front of one of those furnace holes in the rocks. He had been exposed to these caustic, sulphurous gases for many days. It had taken all the oil form his skin, leaving it dry and scaly looking.

The stuff was tearing at Captain Hazzard's throat. He stopped long enough to open one of his belt pouches and slip on the small gas mask he always carried. He never went without it. It had helped in many other adventures. Its scientific respirator, of his own customizing, strained whatever good air there was. As the fumes grew thicker, his life depended on it.

The climb seemed endless. It was an hour before he finally felt the air getting cooler, the fumes thinning. Then at last the flume opened into a horizontal passage. Captain Hazzard flung himself exhausted on the rocks. He took off his gas mask and breathed clean air.

Suddenly, he sat bolt upright. Tautness filled his whole being. His senses were tingling. Those strange psychic whispers of danger to which he was given raced through his mind. Not danger to himself this time, but danger to those for whom he was responsible – danger to Mary Parker and the others left in the jungle cave.

Hazzard stood in up in a frozen trance as his psychic feeling became stronger. He could see now dimly – see the pictures in his mind's eye of what was happening; see Mary Parker, Martin, Jake and Wash being carried tied to poles through the jungle night by the jubilant savages. He saw the dreadful barbaric procession entering the passage to the volcanic stronghold of the Phoenix.

Hazzard broke from his trance and ran along the passage with anxiety clutching his throat like an icy vice. He had to gotten them into this. He had brought them to Guatemala. It was all on his shoulders. Now he must get them out, save them somehow.

But a great earthquake tremor shook the rocks as though to mock his efforts, as though to show the helplessness of one human being in this place of titanic forces.

High above his head in the vaulted roof of the passage, stones loosened and rained down. They crashed at his feet. They made him trip and stumble. He threw up his arms to protect himself, but a good sized chunk struck his forehead and Hazzard pitched forward, still with the vision of calamity before his eyes.

If he died now, all was lost.

The mountain rumbled and rocks continued to fall.

CHAPTER ELEVEN

The Phoenix

Mary Parker had never known such terror. She hung head downward on a long pole slung over the shoulders of two giant Tzutuhiles. Her wrists and ankles were lashed together above the top of the pole with palm fibers that cut cruelly into her soft skin.

All around her were Indians carrying torches. Their hideous faces shone. Their sharp spears gleamed. Their slitted black eyes were filled with venomous hatred as they looked her way. Each had a green jewel in the center of his forehead which seemed like a third baleful eye. Mary felt as if she were trapped in a nightmare from which there was no awakening.

But it was all real.

Behind her, Jake, Martin and Wash were being carried on similar poles. All their equipment dangled from another pole carried by two savages who brought up the rear.

"Jake," Martin Tracey whispered. "How you holding up, old man?"

Since his savage beating, the Montana wrangler had been comatose, and his friends were afraid he might have suffered some internal injuries.

"I've felt lots better, amigo," came the wry response that immediately alleviated all their worries. "Tarnation, those Injuns made me swallow my gum!"

Hearing the cowboy's genuine surliness, the others couldn't help but chuckle – which prompted punches and kicks from their captors. One of the Indians made an exaggerated sign over his own mouth, his miming obvious. Talking was forbidden. To add emphasis to his warning, he gave Tracey another hard kick to the ribs. The prisoners got the message. Still, Mary Parker could not help but be awed by the amazing courage Hazzard's men displayed. To joke in the middle of such dire circumstances spoke volumes about the character of these fellows. As scared as she was, their resilient and unflagging good humor gave her much needed comfort.

The procession was entering the rocky opening in the mountain. The Indians plunged in, walking in single file, and Mary Parker began to choke. There were fumes in the air that stung her throat and face. The place was warm and stifling.

The trek continued up now into the heart of the mountain.

The Indians stopped at last and dropped her and the others joltingly on the floor of a big rock vault that was empty and had no door. They dropped the equipment, too – all but their rifles and automatics. These the Indians took with them as they shuffled out, leaving their prisoners tied.

Martin spoke tensely the instant they had gone. "There's no door," he said. "No way to lock us up...and not even a guard posted. We can get these cords off and make a break. Roll over, Jake, and I'll untie you."

Jake twisted till his hands were close to Martin's fingers. Tracey quickly got the cords loosened. Then, as soon as Jake's hands were free, he untied the others.

Seeing his bruised and battered features, Mary Parker took a small handkerchief from her shorts, wet the tip with her tongue and began to wipe his dirty face gently. Jake was pleasantly embarrassed by her tender ministrations and just stood still, a crooked smile on his tanned mug.

Martin, meanwhile, moved cautiously toward the open entrance of the room, then stopped with a startled exclamation before he reached it.

Something more implacable than any door appeared suddenly

between him and freedom. A wavering, eerie curtain of pulsating light glowed and shimmered from floor to ceiling between two black screens set close against the walls. Wash rushed up beside his ally, putting a restraining hand on his arm and nodded towards the deadly opening.

"The Death Curtain!"

With Wash's urging, Martin backed away, his face contorted in defeat. Then he pointed toward the pile of their knapsacks.

"We've still got the radio! We can get in touch with Randall. We can get him to send out a message that will reach the government in Guatemala just like Cap said. Maybe they'll send help...before it's too late."

The savages hadn't had the wits to remove the small black box. The guns they had recognized and taken, but the radio looked harmless.

Martin crossed the floor and bent over the radio mechanism with feverish haste. It was built for shortwave communication, and was one of the smallest, most compact two-way sets that Hazzard Laboratories had developed. It ran on powerful chemical batteries, with a range of seventy-five miles. Yet it took up a space no larger than a cigar box.

Martin unsnapped the earphones, clipped them on his head. He adjusted the small mouthpiece, clicked the switch and twirled the dials. "MT calling TR," he said. "Calling TR. Come in, TR..."

A thunderous volley of shots drowned out his speech. They came in quick succession. The radio set on the floor began to dance fantastically. Its tubes popped into splinters. Its cabinet split. Its parts flew in all directions as slugs hammered into it.

Martin whirled, dumbfounded. Behind the curtain of light a dim figure stood...a man with a gun.

His face was indistinct until the light thinned a little in its weird ebb and flow. Then Martin glimpsed it.

The features were wizened. The head was shrunken, matted with long stringy hair like a mummy. The nose was hawklike. The skin was cracked by the fumes of the mountain into hideous reptilian scales. The eyes shone with evil intelligence from deep-sunken

"Martin Whirled dumbfounded. Behind the curtain of light a dim figure stood...a man with a gun."

sockets.

The man didn't look quite human. The way his head rested on his shoulders, the way his shoulders humped, gave him the appearance of a hideous vulture. But his thin, colorless lips opened and he spoke in perfect English.

"Four shots, and I didn't miss once. Ha."

There was silence in the enclosure, tense, expectant, till Mary Parker dared, "Who are you?"

The vulture man's evil gaze turned slowly, explored her lithe, shapely body from head to toe. There was a twisted feel to his stare. He spoke finally with a mocking smile shaping his shriveled visage. "Who I am is one of life's riddles," he laughed. "But..." he peered at each of them in turn, shaking now with silent, evil mirth "...you may call me the Phoenix."

The room was hushed again for seconds as all eyes focused on that sinister, skull-like face. The Phoenix! The man who had been responsible for those murders back in New York. The man who had taken Mary Parker's father prisoner and been the cause of their coming south.

The Phoenix touched his chest, lifted his wizened head. Emotion glared in his sunken eyes, when he thundered:

"I am the Phoenix. Like the ancient bird of imperial Egypt, I draw my strength from the living heart of fire. I am the master of Omoxotl, ruler of the great volcano...and I shall become the ruler of the world!"

Words burst suddenly from Mary Parker's lips. She couldn't be silenced any longer. "What have you done with my father and Kurt Gordon?"

"What?" The thoughts of the Phoenix seemed to come back reluctantly from intoxicating vistas of egotistic grandeur. His eyes fixed themselves on the girl again and his harsh, cackling laughter filled the room. "You wish to know what I've done with your father, do you? Well, my dear Miss Parker, yes I know who you are, I'll take you to him and you can see for yourself."

There was something in his tone, something about his words that made the girl whiten. But she moved forward toward the Curtain of

Death, going as close as she dared.

"Not alone, you don't!" Martin Tracey announced, coming up beside her. "I'm coming with her!" he said.

"No," the Phoenix decreed, pointing at Tracey. "I'll let the girl through, but if any of you men tries to follow her, I'll shoot him dead. And you've seen how good my aim is."

Mary Parker turned to Martin. "Please, don't do anything rash on my account. I'll be alright. Really."

He looked into her dazzling blue eyes and saw the resolve she possessed. He took a step back and addressed their captor. "Very well, but if anything happens to her, I'll kill you!"

The Phoenix merely laughed, then he stepped to the side of the room and touched something. The curtain faded and Mary Parker walked through as in a trance. True to their word, none of the others attempted to follow. They read the menace in the Phoenix's eyes. Then the curtain was reactivated, shimmering as before. The villain and the girl moved off together.

Seen close, the Phoenix's features were so horrible that Mary Parker thought she might faint. They were like a shrunken mask of intolerable evil; like all the sins and cruelties of man merged into one hideous face.

The girl kept her eyes averted. She shrank from any contact with that emaciated body. She followed his shuffling footsteps until they came to a small opening in a wall of rock.

"Through there," the Phoenix indicated. "You can see him. The third from the end."

Mary Parker looked and her heart seemed to twist inside her as if it were skewered on a knife. Her eyes widened. Her hands felt cold. She was looking into the cavern where the chained slaves toiled. And the man who labored third from the end nearest her in the row before the fire holes in the floor was her father.

Her father....skeletal, sweating, corpse-like! She knew! She could tell, in spite of the way he had changed. There were steel rings around his ankles, chains attached to them.

Mark Parker called out in a choking voice, "Father, it's Mary! Father...look...it's me, Mary!"

Only for a brief moment did the man turn his head. It was more like a reflex movement than a conscious action. There was absolutely no awareness in his sunken eyes. They were stupid, vacant, glazed.

And Mary Parker broke into a sudden spasm of hysteria. She screamed, all her pent up worries of the past months unleashed in one primal, uncontrollable wailing.

"*Noooooo!*" She turned and in her madness struck at the Phoenix. She clawed like a wildcat at his hideous face with her nails. Violently, with all the strength she could muster, she lashed at him with her tightly clenched fists.

For all the girl's unleashed fury, the Phoenix did not give ground. He merely reeled his torso back from the unexpected beating, a snarl erupting from his throat. Then he struck back.

He slapped her face with blow after blow that sounded like whips cracking. He drove her from him with a ruthless hatred that made his eyes appear demonic. He continued to slap her till she fell on her knees before him, her golden hair streaming, her face white.

Looking down at her, he saw that several buttons from her shirt had been lost and the smooth round tops of her pink bosom heaved beneath him. He bend over, took a handful of her yellow tresses and pulled her backwards. Mary gasped and fell back onto the hard surface of the passage floor. The fiend straddled her and began to paw her lustfully, his claw like hands tearing aside the khaki material to expose her silky white brassiere. Desperately, the girl twisted her head back and forth, trying to fight him off but the monster in human guise seemed possessed of superhuman strength as he took hold of both her wrists. He held them down over her head with one hand, while his free one continued to fondle her breasts with delight.

Then, in the heat of his sexual perversity, the Phoenix suddenly sat up and released his hold on her. A new, cold look came over him and he climbed off hastily, as if she were contagious. Mary Parker sat up, tried to adjust her ruined shirt, at the same time lifting one hand to her smarting cheeks, sobbing softly on the stone floor outside the very room where her father toiled.

The Phoenix, free of his momentary passion, bent over her trembling body like the vulture he resembled – a vulture ready to feast. "This is a man's world, my dear. This mountain is a place where important work is being done. Work, do you hear me?

Important work – work that history will not forget. And you are useless. You are a girl, weak, foolish and a distraction in your tempting looks. Like a modern day Delilah sent to bring about my downfall with lustful dalliances. But I will not succumb to those charms. Nothing will divert me from the task at hand."

Mary Parker ceased her tears and brushed them away. The man was mad, of that she had no doubt, and she would not give him the satisfaction of thinking he had broken her. She was made of sterner stuff.

"Useless, do you hear me?" the Phoenix reiterated, making sure she heard his claims against her. "There is no food for useless mouths in this mountain. But..." he paused as an idea came to him, "...there is a useful way to get rid of you."

The words infiltrated the girl's mental fugue. What was he planning to do with her? The Phoenix went on with grating emphasis.

"My Indians have customs carried down from long-dead ancestors. They are nature worshippers, animists. The beasts, the birds, the reptiles, even the rocks to them are sacred. They have their special fetishes and idols. It will please them to give you to the sacred serpents of Omoxotl, the great white pythons that have lived near the heart of the mountain since long before the coming of Alvarado. For centuries, the Indians have fed them, made living sacrifices to them, thrown their enemies to them so that the wrath of Terror's Shadow might be appeased. But you will be the first white girl given to the White Lords of Omoxotl! To the Indians, it should be a time of special rejoicing."

Now that his words reached the girl's consciousness, she raised her startled, terrified eyes. What was he saying? White pythons? Lords of Omoxotl! She cried out suddenly, gasping in horror, lifting herself to her feet. Taking a deep breath, she squared her shoulders before him, meeting his gaze directly and willing away her fears.

At first the Phoenix was pleased that his words had filled her with fresh terror. There was an inhuman, sadistic light in his eyes. She had struck him, scratched him. But more importantly, she had entranced him, making him give in to the ways of lust. Now, standing defiantly before, chin up, she was silently insulting his megalomaniacal ego. Where her fear had been a balm to him, her courage was infuriatingly irritating.

"Your bravado won't last, my dear. Not when you look into the pit and see the hundreds of waiting snakes below. They like only living things," he said gloatingly, "warm flesh, still quivering."

Mary Parker looked at him and spoke. "Go to hell!" Then she spat in his frightening face.

The Phoenix's eyes doubled and he slammed his right fist into her chin, knocking her cold. She fell in a heap at his feet.

"Vixen," he fired back. "We'll see who gets to hades first!" He turned and motioned to two of his Indian guards. They rushed over, took hold of the sleeping Mary Parker and proceeded to carry her back to the prison chamber. The Phoenix summoned other men with chains and followed.

When the two Indians carrying Mary Parker neared the shimmering electrical barrier, Martin spotted them first, as he had been worried about the lovely blond all the while she was gone.

"Wash...Jake," he said, alerting his companions. "Look, they've got Mary. And she's hurt!" Then he sighted the Phoenix approaching with the other guards and almost stepped into the Death Curtain, so seething was in the rage in his blood.

"You monster!" he cried, pointing past the death veil. "What did you do to her?"

"That is no concern of yours, my would-be hero," the Phoenix declared, thumping his own chest with his hand. "I am the master of this mountain. My will is law here. The girl dared to defy me, and I had to teach her a lesson."

"Why you cretin, I'll tear you apart with my bare hands!" Tracey threatened, only to be pulled away from the lethal curtain by his companions.

"Stop it," Wash whispered in his ear. "This does neither Mary or us any good. We've got to bide our time, Tracey. And it will come, trust me."

The young doctor looked from the comatose girl to the scientist.

Finally, he ceased his struggling and the men released him. The Phoenix was satisfied he had come to his senses and so pointed out the heavy chains his guards were carrying.

"We have these always available," he said cruelly. "The work is such that the workers fall by the way, making room for others. There is no unemployment problem in Omoxotl!"

Hazzard's three aides were frustrated and out-flanked. They never once considered making a break for it as the Phoenix switched off the light curtain to allow his men to bring in Mary Parker. A dozen Indians with knives, clubs and spears stood grimly in the doorway, ready to pounce if they even sneezed threateningly. To fight now would be suicidal, and nothing would be gained by throwing away their lives. And they knew Captain Hazzard would not condone such a futile sacrifice. Mysterious psychic forces told them that he was still alive somewhere. The only way they could help him, and help themselves, was to do what Wash had said – wait until some opportunity presented itself.

As the Indians lay Mary Parker on the floor, Martin balled his hands into fists, but kept them at his side. Jake also gritted his teeth at the sight of the bruised and helpless girl.

As they stood rigid, the Phoenix's braves began to affix the heavy chains to their legs. There was a fearful finality about the feel of the steel rings on their ankles. With the Indians walking beside them, holding spears against their bodies, the trio were taken away. As they shuffled down the long passage, Tracey took one last look at the supine form in the makeshift jail. He was in time to see the Phoenix switch on the Death Curtain again.

They were taken directly to the room with the furnace-like holes.

Two places were empty, and at the third a slave had collapsed. His head lolled horribly askew. His mouth was open. His tongue, black and swollen, was thrust through cracking lips. He was dead, killed by the fearful labor, and his body was removed to make room for Jake to take his place.

The Phoenix had come in, too. He looked on coolly while the Indians chained the new slaves in the toiling row. The others hadn't stopped their work for a moment. They held long ladle-like implements. They thrust these into the fire cavities with some of the brownish rocks in them. Every few minutes they drew the ladles out, plunged them into a vat of liquid for a second, then thrust them back into the holes again. They kept this up till the rocks turned black. Then they dumped the rocks to one side and began again with fresh ones.

Jake was given one of the long-handled ladles, together with a chunk of rock. He was told by the Phoenix to copy the movements of the workers. Indians dressed in hideous python skins, clutching long whips, stood around with masklike faces.

Jake knew they were there to keep the slaves busy. But he was curious about the rocks and ladles. He stared at the Phoenix, pointed to his chunk of rock. "What's that for?" he boldly asked.

"Questions are forbidden!" the Phoenix barked. He made a quick gesture. The nearest Python Man brought his whip down on Jack's unprotected back in a blow that cut the skin deeply. Jake sucked in a breath, but did not wince. He thrust his ladle sullenly into the fire and whispered to Wash, who was chained close by: "I'd rather be a horned toad in hell than fork my fuzztail permanent with this herd of sour-bellies."

CHAPTER TWELVE

Altar of the Python Men

The next twenty-four hours went by tortuously slow for the three Americans pressed into hard labor in the mountain's natural furnace. Wash, Martin and Jake all toiled in silence, ever under the watchful scrutiny of the armed sentries. Still, each of them clung, individually, to the hope that Captain Hazzard was alive.

Martin, because he was related to Hazzard by blood, was the one with the strongest psychic bond. Thus he displayed no outward reaction when he at long last received a familiar mental signal from his cousin.

"Martin, are you alright?" The unspoken words flitted through his consciousness. Without breaking his stride in the ladling process, the young surgeon mentally transmitted his reply, at the same instant inquiring as to Hazzard's present condition.

Through this telepathic exchange, both men were able to ascertain the events that had transpired as if they were looking through the other's eyes.

Martin learned that Hazzard was still lost in the maze-like passages of Omoxotl. Upon regaining consciousness from the blow to the head, Hazzard had spent hours of desperate searching, exploring air flumes and narrow crevices – hours of sounding the lava walls for possible spots where an opening might be made.

All of which bore little result. He was still lost. Whereas through Martin's thoughts, Captain Hazzard witnessed the capture of the his friends and their imprisonment in the rock chamber. Through Martin's visualization, he got an impression of the Phoenix – someone of a personality more fiend than man. Of Mary Parker, he knew that she had gone out from the cell to see her father and had been brought back in a faint, her clothes virtually in tatters. He also fully experienced Martin's red-hot anger at the sight of the sweet girl's condition and how he had nearly dared the Curtain of Death to get his hands on the Phoenix.

Now briefed, he saw his team chained and working in the very same cavern he had spied earlier. Since Martin had no inkling of the fearful fate in store for Mary Parker, he could neither instruct Hazzard.

Stay strong," Captain Hazzard sent. "Tell the others the same and that I will come for you."

To which Martin Tracey responded through the ether, "Will do. Be careful, Cap!"

Of course, neither Martin or anyone else could help him with his immediate problem. That was to find a way of the tomb-like rock cavern in which he was trapped.

He had tried almost everything. He had burned smoke powders and watched the way the vapor drifted in an effort to discover hidden drafts that might lead to concealed openings. He had found several of these, but they had been only minute cracks. In sheer desperation he climbed as high as he could get on one side of the wall. As he climbed, he swept his flashlight over the ceiling.

It was thus that he discovered a small black fissure in the roof of the vault. Did it lead to another, higher chamber, or was it merely a pocket created by a falling rock? Hazzard didn't know. But at the risk of a bone-shattering plunge, he climbed up to it. Reaching out from a narrow ledge, he thrust his arm in the black air pocket.

Excitement gripped him instantly. There was a faint draft there.

Tensely, he took one of the small bombs from his belt. He set its chemical fuse to the maximum explosion point of five minutes, then wedged it tightly into the fissure. He wasn't sure it would give him time to get down, but he had to risk it. He descended hastily, taking long chances. At the last, as seconds flew by, he jumped to the stone floor from a height of thirty feet, bending his knees as he landed to break the shock. The instant he hit, he turned and fled down the passage and swung himself flat behind the first turn.

The explosion overhead filled the corridor with shattering, ear-splitting echoes that reverberated throughout. Showers of rock came down. Great boulders fell a few feet behind him. And after the explosion, Hazzard's pulse was racing.

For there was now a gaping hole in the roof, a black opening large enough to admit his body. He climbed up once more, squeezed through the space he'd blasted, and found himself in another chamber. There was a tight feeling around his heart as he ran along it. Since the mountain was honeycombed with passages, this might be a blind one, too.

But a faint glow appeared ahead at the end of five minutes. Daylight this time! Daylight after hours of wandering in darkness. The sight of that opening in the rocks gave Captain Hazzard new vigor.

He crept forward cautiously. He wasn't sure where he was yet, or when he might run into patrolling savages. But as soon as he reached the natural gap, he saw that caution for the moment was needless. He was far up on the side of the great peak. Below him was the gorge through which he'd followed the Indian the night before. Spreading out was a vast panorama of the jungle, with the Espiritu Santo range on the far horizon. Hazzard began moving along a narrow ledge on the face of the mountain. He carefully put one foot before the other, moving at a snail's pace. Where the ledge widened, he increased his descent, skillfully climbing down toward a spot where he had glimpsed what appeared to be another passage mouth.

But it still took time to reach it. The going was harder than he had expected. He had to slip down the bare face of the rock in certain spots where the ledge was non-existent. Here he hung on precariously. When he did get near the opening, he paused abruptly and listened.

From out of that cave-like maw in the rock came weird, barbaric music, the sound of many voices, wailing, chanting. It seemed far off, ghostly. It rose and fell. It had a persistent rhythm. And to Hazzard, who was sensitive to the tones and moods of even the most primitive races, there was in it a note of unearthly horror.

****

Mary Parker, too, heard that chanting. But it wasn't far away from her. It didn't reach her ears through hundreds of feet of rocky passage. It was all around her. In front...in back...beside her, beating against her eardrums in wave upon wave of shuttering dread.

It seemed to be bearing her along on an evil tide of sound. But it was the Indians themselves who carried her. She wasn't slung beneath a pole now. She sat on a royal couch-like litter of ocelot skin trimmed with the waving plumes of the sacred quetzal.

She, too, was dressed in the bright green feathers. She wore a smock of them over her own silky underwear. Upon coming to in the prison chamber, the Tzutuhiles had made her disrobe and put this feathery garment on her slender, hour-glass figure. It hung from her creamy white shoulders to the just below her thighs, exposing her long, elegant, bare legs. Over her lustrous blonde hair they had slipped a band of gleaming gold ornamented with a bright green jewel. It was the sacred emerald of the Tzutuhiles, the flawless gem that came from the rocks of this wild country. She was being borne along like a queen in state. Four chanting Python Men held the corners of her litter.

But her hands and feet were bound. She was not a queen in reality, but a human sacrifice on her way to serve her awful masters.

She knew who these masters were. The Phoenix, during his verbal abuse, had told her. She knew, and yet her mind could not fathom a thing of such unspeakable horror. It shied away from it, drew back dazed, dared not even contemplate it. Twice in the past few minutes she had nearly fainted away.

But close at hand, bringing that horror home to her, was an Indian with hands bound and head bent walking just ahead of her litter. He must have sinned against the Phoenix, she guessed. The quivering features of his face, the look in his eyes, stabbed like sharp blades across her nerve fibers. The masters whom she went to serve were to have him too.

The procession move on singing, carrying torches in the dim catacombs of the mountain. Mary Parker sat on the litter with a white face and eyes dark with steadily mounting dread.

They came at last to a chamber that was roofed high like an old world cathedral. There was a rocky floor in front. Toward the back the floor ended sharply, giving way to a steep-sided pit. In the air of this expansive room was a faint, musky scent that made the girl's body tremble.

The singing ceased in a moment. The Python Men ranged themselves around the edge of the pit. In the silence that followed, Mary Parker heard a slithering, scraping whisper of sound that was hateful, spine-chilling.

Drawn by a morbid fascination that was stronger than will, she turned her head and stared down when the Python Men brought her close to the edge of the pit.

There under the light of the flaring torches, she glimpsed the scaled white coils of the giant snakes. They were moving slowly, curling, unwinding, writhing over each other – a squirming, horrible mass of giant pythons, bleached almost to a milky whiteness because the sun had not touched them or their ancestors for untold ages.

They thrust their great heads up. They glared with their cold green eyes. Their forked tongues flickered. Their scaly necks swayed, dropped back, rose again.

The Indians took their bound former comrade and suddenly hurled him down into the pit among those writhing, twisting reptilian bodies.

It had happened so fast, Mary Parker's already frayed mind reeled. She dropped forward on the litter, shielding her eyes, stifling the scream caught in her throat.

But she couldn't shout out the awful sounds that came up from the pit. She couldn't close her ears to those hideous, pitiful cries, those snappings and crunchings. It was only when the sounds reached their climax, when two of the great pythons had thrown their coils tightly around the Indian's body and were crushing the life out of him, that Mary Parker again mercifully swooned into oblivion.

When the preparations for the horrible feast in the pit began, when one of the pythons drew into a corner with his human prey to crush it and knead it, Mary lay unconscious on the litter. She didn't feel the rough savage hands that clutched her limp figure and raised her slowly aloft.

Then the chanting started anew. A high priest of the animist cult lifted the green jewel from Mary's forehead. They held it up on a feathered arrow, walked it to the serpent pit and made several mystic passes.

The pythons thrust their ghostly heads up again as it their cold brains told them another victim was to be thrown to them. These walls had echoed to that strange chanting often before. Never had it failed to mean food for the reptiles.

The chanting was louder, deeper, more fervent. The priests were shaking visibly with an emotion close to madness as they lifted Mary Parker and carried her slowly to the edge of the pit.

CHAPTER THIRTEEN

Hell's Control Room

Then it happened – a thing that made the Python Men freeze into rigid statues of fear. A light glowed suddenly in the middle of the serpent pit – a light as bright as a ruby and as red as blood. It flared out of the semi-darkness, making the pythons hiss and slither away.

The Indians hadn't heard the faint stir of the tiny cone that sailed over their heads. They hadn't seen it in their preoccupation with the awful ceremony being enacted.

It had landed on a python's writhing, rubbery body which deadened the sound when it fell. An instant after landed, it burst into flame, spurting red fire at its narrow tip. And now it was burning weirdly, fearfully to the Indian's eyes. In its glow, the white pythons seemed to be bathed in blood.

The Indians drew back staring. The mysterious red light seemed to imply that Omoxotl was angry for some reason. Its sudden appearance was a clear sign that they had done something wrong.

And as they stood transfixed with supernatural awe, staring at that strange blood-rouge fire, something moved across the stone floor behind them, rolling almost to their feet.

It came to rest finally close to the edge of the precipice.

It was a silvery ball about the size of an egg. There were perforations in it. As it rolled, a slender black cord hardly thicker than a thread unwound from it, and trailed behind it into the shadows.

When the Python Men at last looked down and noticed the silver egg, they failed to see the cord. They didn't know where the odd shiny ball had come from or what it was. They stared stupidly from it to the flare in the pit.

Then a sound rose from their very feet – a thin, haunting voice, as though some spectral being dwelt in the floor of the room.

"Nihongi! Nihongi!" It was one of several words common to most of the Indian dialects of Guatemala. "Nihongi!" the voice said again. "Go!" Then the voice rose till it seemed to fill the whole chamber. "Leave the maiden! Go! Or die!"

A superstitious lot, the Indians broke into a wild stampede of terror. With contorted faces, waving arms, rolling eyes they turned from the pythons' pit and fled toward the exit portal. The damning, blood-red glow of the strange fire seemed to follow them. Their panic increased with every step they took. Omoxotl was angry. Omoxotl had spoken. They had seen his fiery orb. They had heard his chilling voice. He has spurned their sacrificial offering.

They bolted through the door of the room, yelling, clawing, knocking each other down, trailing green feathers. They let their torches fall and sputter. In a surging, frenzied human wave, they turned left and rushed down the long rock corridor up which they had come.

As the sound of their thudding feet diminished, a shadow detached itself from the dark recess at the right of the door. A tall figure strode quickly into the sacred pythons' room.

It was Captain Hazzard, and he went at once to the prostrate girl. He bent over her, saw her chest rising and falling and knew she was still alive. Before picking her up, he paused long enough to rewind the black cord on the tiny spheroid loudspeaker that had saved her life. It was made of aluminum, light as a feather, but could amplify the human voice to a level many times greater than its usual volume.

Hazzard had developed it, together with a buttonhole microphone, as a means of communication with friends or assistants in out-of-the-way places. The spheroid speaker slipped easily into one of the pouches of his wide leather belt.

He lifted feather-weight girl in his strong arms, then turned and moved quickly out of the room and strode after the fleeing Python Men. There was no time to lose. When they told the Phoenix what had happened, the Phoenix would grow suspicious and start an investigation. But if Hazzard could reach the part of the mountain where the Phoenix maintained his headquarters, there might be a chance to make some investigations of his own while the panic-stricken savages held their master's attention. It would take the Phoenix some minutes to convince them Oxomotl wasn't angry.

As he jogged along, Hazzard was all too aware of the warm bundle in his powerful arms. With his right arm about her ribs and holding her against his chest, his left was hooked about her long, bare legs and he was acutely aware of their satiny feel. He also saw the many welts that the red ants had inflicted on her smooth, flawless skin, amid the dirt and scratches she had endured in the past few days.

The ever-present lilac scented perfume tickled his nostrils as her head rocked back and forth on his collarbone, her golden hair brushing against his neck. She was a beautiful young woman who had endured a great ordeal in her quest to save her father. Hazzard admired her pluck and her courage, but he was also well aware of her enticing beauty. But those kinds of thoughts were for later, in a more civilized place and time. For now, his entire being was focused on defeating their diabolical foe and surviving the next few hours.

He broke into a full run, swinging the girl in his embrace. The sound of the Indians was far away now. Burdened as he was, he couldn't expect to catch up. But he kept them within earshot, ran down gloomy, twisting passages, crossed natural vaults in the mountain. Some few of the savages had clung to their torches. When the passage was straight, he could see their glow and his helped him to follow.

Mary stirred in his arms presently. The draft on her face was reviving her. Even though she was unconscious, the magnetic aura of Captain Hazzard's brain and body seemed to be driving the clouds of horror and depression from her mind.

By the time they reached the level of the chamber where the chained slaves toiled, Mary's eyes were open. Hazzard come closer to the torch wielders. In their light, Mary Parker got a glimpse of his handsome profile. Her hands clutched him. Her voice came in a thin whisper like someone waking from a nightmare.

"Captain Hazzard! Is it really you?" There was both hope and disbelief with a touch of amazement in her voice.

He nodded, never slowing his easy gait, then said in a low voice: "You've had a rough go of it, Miss Parker. Rest easy, collect your wits and then let me know when you feel strong enough to walk."

She said nothing for a few minutes. Her body relaxed and she seemed to sink into another trance. He could only guess at how weak she must feel after those moments of unforgettable horror. It was an ordeal few women – and even some men – could suffer and remain sane.

Suddenly she roused herself, looked about and said, "I can walk now."

He wasn't sure of it, but he let her slip to the floor gently. In an instant, again to his surprise, she was running along beside him.

"Hurry!" she whispered. "I've seen my father. He's here...alive."

"I know," he answered, causing her to stare at him for a brief second. The question as to how was on her face. "Tracey sent me a telepathic message."

"Then you know they're torturing him, and those other poor devils. They'll die if we don't save them. We must!"

"And we shall, I promise you. Now we mustn't talk. Simply follow my lead in whatever happens next."

The Python Men had paused now. He could see their torches flaring down at the end of a long rock corridor. He could hear their voices jabbering. They must be clamoring outside the private chambers of the Phoenix to tell him of the dread thing that had happened. Here was the opportunity for which he had hoped.

He moved stealthily toward the frenzied group of green-robed

Tzutuhiles. Other Indians were coming from all directions, slipping out of doors and passages, running to see what the excitement was all about.

As one door opened, Hazzard caught a glimpse of a big, lighted room filled with strange machinery. When the Indian wearing a white lab smock had come out of the room, he disappeared in the direction of the yelling group, Hazzard whispered:

"This way. Come!"

His army automatic was in his right hand now. In his left was another of the walnut-size bombs. As a last resort, he stood ready to fling it if he encountered trouble. Mary Parker pressed in close behind him trying to see past his shoulder. But the big room was virtually empty except for one man, a slave chained before a long work table strewn with delicate instruments.

The man raised startled eyes. He was Teutonic in appearance, small, intelligent looking with a blond-bearded face. There was long suffering etched on his features, deep-seated fear in his small brown eyes. He looked at Hazzard and the girl as though he saw two ghosts.

Hazzard cautioned him by putting his finger to his lips. The fellow understood the situation at a glance. Here was one of the Phoenix's trained technicians. A great brain probably, a scientist or scholar who had somehow fallen into the madman's hands. The Phoenix made slaves of civilized men, chained them, worked them to death under the cruel whips of his barbarous Python Men.

Hazzard spoke to the bearded worker in English and the man answered with a Germanic accent: "Vat iss it you are doing here? Und der fraulein! Do you not know de Venix vill kill you! Get oudt from here...run vile you still can!"

In clipped sentences, Hazzard, speaking fluent German, told the prisoner who he was and what had happened, and he saw hope flare in the chained man's eyes. The man said his name was Otto Beckhardt. He was a chemist working for a mining company and had been captured by the Tzutuhiles, then brought here.

While the frail scientist rambled, Mary Parker moved about the expansive lab, her natural curiosity piqued. In a back corner she found a steel locker from which she took a lab smock and put it on over her skimpy dress of jade feathers.Buttoning the front of the jacket, she spotted several pairs of rubber-soled lap slippers. Luckily the Phoenix's staff of natives were small men whose shoe sizes were a near match for her own dainty limbs. Once in the coat and shoes, the modest girl felt a renewed confidence. She sauntered back to the big table where Beckhardt was waving his short arms and crying hoarsely.

"Der Venix iss mad...mad vid a crazy ego dat makes him vant to rule der vorld." He had been using his pidgin English for so long, he could not break the habit. "But he iss a great genius. Look about you!"

Hazzard stared around the magnificent lab with its strange assortment of machines festooned with levers of all sizes and shapes. Dials, huge metal coils and giant valves were everywhere he looked. The lab resembled a power substation one would find in a great metropolis instead of a chamber deep in the heart of a volcano. It was incredible, the work of a great mind, a mighty energy. There were whirring dynamos, electric lights, huge switchboards. But what of the power to run all this?

Hazzard guessed the startling secret even before Beckhardt stabbed one stubby finger dramatically at the floor. "Down dere. All of it! Dere in der volcano's heart!"

That was the answer. The Phoenix had harnessed the subterranean fires of Omoxotl. Hazzard knew that many daring engineers from around the globe had proposed such a thing. They had theorized in scientific papers that there was enough power in the average volcano, enough heat units to run a mighty modern city for hundreds of years. But no one had dared act upon the idea – no one except the Phoenix. It had taken a half-crazed brain, a man obsessed with limitless ambition, a man who held human life cheaply. It had taken a personality that was half genius and half fiend.

Captain Hazzard stepped to the wall of the room where hung a huge diagram in a frame. It was a diagram of Omoxotl, showing the course of the crater, its depth and structure. And here before Hazzard's startled eyes were details of the vast engineering operation.

The Phoenix had thrown a giant valve across the crater, five hundred feet below its summit. He had capped the volcano, controlling the mighty gas pressure, just as lesser engineers cap oil wells.

Steel girders such as those used to build bridges had been set in the rock, reinforced, roofed over with other girders and plates of steel riveted together. The valve in the center was worked by a system of giant worm gears operated by an electric turbine.

Hazzard shuddered when he considered the toll of human life that this vast project must have taken. How many workers had fallen screaming into the fiery bowels of the mountain? How many others had perished in the stifling gases? And how many thousands, how many millions of dollars had this undertaking cost?

Mary Parker came over and stood beside him. The look of concentration on Hazzard's face was intense. It was clear to her that his mind was swiftly absorbing the wonders of what he was learning.

"What is it, Captain? What does it all stand for?"

Without taking his eyes from the detailed schematic, he said, "We are looking at an engineering miracle to compare with the great pyramids of Egypt."

Hazzard's excited gaze continued to run over the design, comparing it with the machinery in the room. He saw the delicate instruments under a glass case that made second-by-second recordings of the pressure of the subterranean gases. He saw that it operated a safety control attached to the great central worm gear.

This gear was in ceaseless motion, opening and closing the massive valve, letting gas escape or shutting it in, to keep the pressure constant. It could be varied by a rheostat. Except for this, the mountain might blow up, or the pressure that the Phoenix needed in his work might vanish if the subterranean fires sank below a certain point.

Then Hazzard saw another control, another series of lines on the diagram. These showed how the pressure could be increased by allowing water from an underground river to fall into the crater.

The water turned to live steam before it struck bottom. The steam turned to superheated gases.

Hazzard tensed suddenly as his mind grasped what would happen if the one control was closed and the other opened. He remembered the great volcano, Krakatoa, in the strait of Sundra, near Java. Sea water had fallen into Krakatoa's crate and it had erupted with an appalling loss of life, blowing a whole island to bits and filling the atmosphere of the entire earth with dust motes. Yes, the Phoenix was playing with forces so great that they staggered the imagination.

And what of his light-wave Death Curtain? Hazzard spoke to Beckhardt about it. The German chemist shrugged. "I do no know," he said. "Only der Venix knows. But dere are pabers...dere in dat safe iff one could open it. Dere are plans showing it. Maybe iff..."

But Hazzard had already darted away. He was kneeling before the safe, moving the dials, listening to the tumblers. He must have more knowledge. Their lives might depend on what he learned in the few moments left to him. Mary Parker watched him and recalled MacGowen's words concerning Hazzard's obsession with knowledge. It was being played out before her now, and once again she marveled at the man who had come into her life at just the right time. He truly was a modern-day knight who lived by a high moral code of chivalry and honor.

Hazzard took a silencer from a belt pouch and screwed it over the barrel of his automatic. He started to lay the gun on the floor beside him. He would shoot – and shoot to kill if he were interrupted.

Mary Parker, blue eyes wide, came over and offered him assistance, indicating the weapon. "Can I be of any help?"

Hazzard looked up at her and then smiled. He handed her the 45. "Go to the door and stand guard. If anyone comes, don't hesitate to use this."

"I won't."

Hefting the pistol, the girl went to take her position by the door. Meanwhile, Hazzard returned to the safe dial. In a few minutes he had it open. His hands pulled out a stack of papers and began shuffling through them. Then he found it, exactly what he wanted. He ran across the room to Beckhardt and together they examined the papers. But Beckhardt could make nothing of them. He simply did not have the vast training nor the technical background of Wash MacGowen.

"Hazzard was kneeling before the safe, moving the dials, listening to the tumblers."

It was Hazzard himself who understood these blueprints and complex mathematical figures. Wash had been right in assuming the thing might be atomic. The Phoenix had used the power of Omoxotl to break down individual atoms into their component electrons. Sending the electrons into space on alpha rays from a Roentgen tube, he had built up an atomic barrage of deadly power, a protoplasmic oxidizer that congealed the blood and brought death quickly. It was a thing of horror, of far-reaching consequences.

And there was literature in the safe to show that the Phoenix intended to develop this into a weapon that would make the nations of the world bow to his will. Through his network of agents, he was corresponding even now with certain European governments. He hadn't let the secret out of his hands as yet, but he had drawn up plans to turn the entire world into one vast corporate state with headquarters in Omoxotl and himself as supreme dictator.

Here was the dream of a megalomaniac – but a dream that could spread untold misery and horror if it wasn't nipped in the bud. Hazzard knew that the small light machines tried out in New York and in the air were only the beginning.

Mary Parker called out a warning. "Someone's coming!"

She flattened herself against the wall near the door. A moment later, the native wearing the lab smock walked through. He saw Hazzard with Beckhardt and froze in amazement. He opened his mouth to shout.

Mary Parker brought the barrel of the automatic down on the Indian's skull with a loud crack. He groaned softly and fell over. Hazzard raced over. "Good work, " he said, and the girl nodded and went back to watching the outside corridor.

Hazzard pulled the body across the room and deposited it behind the big steel lockers. But not before searching the Indian's pockets. In these he found a set of keys on a ring, one of which unlocked the shackles on Beckhardt's ankles.

Beckhardt came forward, a slave no longer, with deep-heartfelt gratitude shining in his small blue eyes. Hazzard thrust one of his tiny, deadly bombs into the chemist's hand. He showed him how to use it, then said, "Stay here...you and Miss Parker. Don't use that bomb unless you have to. But use it if you must to save yourselves from recapture."

"Und vare are you going, my friend?"

"To try and free the other slaves."

At the door, Hazzard gave Mary Parker her instructions. "In case anything should happen to me, you'll be on your own."

She understood. "Yes." She held up the automatic, her eyes hard with resolve. "I'll save a bullet...if they try to take me back to that pit..." and her voice trailed off, recalling the horror of the snakes.

Hazzard had no doubt she would. Nothing could make her face that nightmarish horror again.

"Have faith," he said. "We'll win out yet."

He looked out, saw that all was clear and stepped swiftly into the passage. Moving as stealthily as a shadow, he hurried along the dark corridor toward the room where the slaves toiled.

As he went, his mind was sending out calls to Wash and Tracey, telling them to get ready for action.

CHAPTER FOURTEEN

The Fury of Omoxotl

"Careful, Kevin," the mental warning blared in his mind as he surreptitious approached the main work cavern. "The Phoenix has posted more guards!"

Captain Hazzard recognized Wash MacGowen's peculiar mental fingerprints. He slowed his steps and slowly sidled up to the main corridor leading to the entrance. He could hear the noise of the chain gangs up ahead. Peering around a rock corner, he spied the biggest native guard ever. The huge man was standing in front of the main entryway, garbed in the python-skin hood and holding a steel-shafted spear.

"Get ready to cause a ruckus," Hazzard sent MacGowen. Everything had to happen fast or he would lose the crucial element of surprise. There was no time for finesse.

Other savages were already drifting back to their posts throughout the mountain. The group of Tzutuhiles who had fled from the python pit in terror were coming out of the Phoenix's private chamber with their frenzy calmed. In another few minutes, Hazzard knew that the Phoenix would begin an investigation of the weird episode at the pit.

In another few minutes, every savage in the vast catacombs would be warned and alert.

Hazzard flung himself recklessly on the tall, armed sentry. He hoped to knock him out, quiet him, and grab his spear before any of the other guards in the chamber came running.

But for once, Hazzard had underestimated the lightning rapidity of savage reflexes. As well try to take a dozing jaguar by surprise as one of these grim Tzutuhiles.

The man turned in a flash of a split-second, before Hazzard's hands had even touched his body. Like the claw of a striking cat, the spear flashed out. The Indian snarled deep in his throat and Hazzard leaped aside as the spear point brushed him. Its steel blade sliced his shirt. He felt the Indian's hot breath on his face.

At the same time, several of the other guards, hearing the commotion at the front, started to respond. Seeing them move for the entrance, MacGowen signaled Jake and Tracey with his hands.

As the guards walked past, the trio pulled their ankle chains around so as to trip up the natives. Then as the Indians stumbled, fell into each other, the Americans went at them as best they could, fists flying.

Seeing the brave Americans attacking their armed guards, those laborers whose will had not been totally subjugated shook off their mental lethargy and joined in, falling on the outnumbered Python Men with blood-curdling yells. Within seconds, the slave revolt of Omoxotl was underway.

Captain Hazzard struck at the seven-foot-tall guard's helmeted face with a hard right and connected with the Indian's jaw. The blow would have felled a regular opponent, but it failed even to stun the big savage. The Tzutuhile let out an angry roar. Head down, he came at Hazzard with the spear again. In the background, Hazzard could hear the melee going on inside and knew his men had jumped into the fray. But chained as they were, they would soon be at the mercy of the armed Indians, no matter how well they fought.

Desperate to aid them, Hazzard took a chance and gave ground for a moment before the spearman. He spun around just as the Indian drove the point forward to spear his chest. His hand flashed and caught the lance just as it shot by him. He gave it a savage tug, jerking the giant off-balance, then tripped him and sent him sprawling to the floor face-first.

Hazzard wrenched the spear from the fallen man's grip and smacked him on the back of the head with it. Suddenly, another guard emerged from the chamber and came at him like a raging beast. Hazzard parried the guard's spear with his own, then smashed across the native's forehead, downing him instantly.

Without any further delay, he raced into the main work area in time to see one of the guards about to skewer Martin Tracey, on his knees entangled with his own chain. Hazzard hurled the guard's spear and it caught the would-be killer in the back, ripping through his chest. Hazzard raced over to the dead Indian and examined his clothing.

"Thanks, Kevin," Tracey said, a tired smile on his face.

"My pleasure, Martin." He fished out a ring of keys from the dead guard and unlocked his cousin's ankle bracelet. Then he tossed the keys to MacGowen, who with Jake Cole had just beaten two guards senseless. "Here, Wash. Get free and then start freeing the others!"

Using a duplicate key, Hazzard went to the far side of the room and deftly, knowing they only had a few minutes at best, began unlocking the chains from the slaves. He was the first to reach Mary's father.

Franklin Parker and some of the other slaves took a few stumbling steps and collapsed at their sudden freedom. It was too much for them after the routine they had so long endured.

"Help, them, men!" ordered Hazzard. "Those of you capable of walking lend a hand to the others. Quick, follow me. We've got to the protection of the control room."

Wash, Jake and Tracey each took hold of a hapless slave and held him up. Walking in this fashion would be slow going, but the alternative was to leave them behind – something no one on Hazzard's team would ever consider. They would die before giving up one of these wretched fellows to the Phoenix. Again they were an example to the others who, immediately, upon being released from their chains, went to the aid of their companions.

In total, they numbered thirty-three. Most were obviously Guatemalan, but Hazzard recognized half a dozen caucasian slaves in the group and assumed, like Beckhardt, they were foreign agents who all shared the misfortune of crossing the Phoenix's path. He wondered which of them was Parker's partner, Kurt Gordon. But now was not the time for formal introductions.

By now Captain Hazzard had picked up Mary Parker's exhausted father and draped him over his left shoulder in a fireman's carry. Hazzard was appalled at how little the man weighed.

A mad, desperate plan was shaping itself in Hazzard's brain. He must reach the control room of the lost city again. He must have Wash there to help him.

Already the noise of their fighting had attracted attention.

As he stepped into the main corridor, three more Indians came running toward him. They paused only an instant. Then, with shrill cries, leaped forward brandishing their spears. Jake, Wash and Martin, aiding the feeble slaves, were within their easy reach.

Hazzard flung pellets of tear gas which hindered the Indians' onrush, but didn't stop it. With streaming eyes and distorted faces they came through it. They hurled themselves on Hazzard and the others. For a moment there was a mad, hand-to-hand conflict.

Encumbered by his human burden, Captain Hazzard fought defensively and managed to drop two of the Tzutuhiles with quick Jujitsu kicks. Jake dropped the slave he was helping in the melee and retaliated by getting one of the spears away from one of his attackers. He spun the long pole like a majorette's baton then slapped the former owner across the face.

"*Yahooo*," he howled like a mule driver. "Come an' git it! Lots more where that came from!"

Hazzard knocked a second savage out with a short, powerful punch to the man's sternum. Just then another Indian threw his spear and it caught one next to Wash in the neck. It pierced him, almost sliced his head from his body. Blood splashed over Wash's arm as the man, who moments before had relished the hope of freedom, went down with his troubles ended forever.

Hazzard plunged on along the passage, realizing they could not win a prolonged engagement of this ferocity. The others followed after him. They reached the door of the control room as a howling mob of Indians, aware now that a break had been made by the slaves, came charging from the direction of the Phoenix's headquarters.

Mary Parker yanked open the door and moved out of the way quickly. Dozens of spears whistled through the air even before Hazzard had marshalled his troops through the control room door.

When the last man was in, he slammed the door shut and shoved the deadbolt home.

He had noticed the deadbolt before leaving. It was part of his plan.

Hazzard next walked to the middle of the control lab and gently, with Mary Parker's help, lay her father on the floor.

"Father!" she exclaimed, recognizing him immediately. "Is he alright?"

"Just weak from malnutrition," Hazzard answered. "See if there's any water in here. For him and the others."

As the girl, along with Jake and Tracey, saw to the well being of the freed men, Hazzard turned to Wash and explained briefly what he had discovered about the Death Curtain. While the Indians beat on the door, he showed Wash the plans he had taken from the safe.

Wash knitted his brows as calmly as though death were not howling outside. "Amazing," he said. "Extraordinary. You were right, Kevin, I shouldn't have been afraid to follow any line of reasoning, however wild it might seem. This thing utilizes the force released from the breakdown of atoms. The force is discharged between two terminals and carried on alpha rays. We shall have to call in the quantum theory to explain it."

Wash was once again a college professor giving a lecture, so absorbed in his subject now that he had forgotten all about their current state of jeopardy. Hazzard brought him back to reality.

"I know Wash," he said tensely. "It's atomic, all right. Alpha rays are the carrying agent. The point is, can we build up a defense against it?"

"I don't know," admitted Wash. "It would take some research."

"Research!" Hazzard laughed grimly. "There is an army of Indians out there waiting to do research with spears to find out what our innards are made of. No, Wash. We've got to act quickly. We've got to take a chance."

"But how...?"

"Look. We've got to break down the polarization of the carrying agent. We can't hope to touch the atomic factor itself. We don't know enough about it. But mightn't we blast through it, upset the polarization with a dose of the same poison? I mean, use more alpha rays to cut through and bisect the carriers?"

Dawning comprehension made Wash's eyes glow brightly. He rubbed his long chin excitedly. "It's possible, Kevin...barely possible. But even that would take time. We'd have to have an X-ray outfit."

"Over here," directed Hazzard. "But it's too big to carry. We need something portable. Can you strip it down, Wash, make it lighter and still have it work?"

"Time," repeated Wash. "I can do most anything...given time."

"There is no time," snapped Captain Hazzard, his patience depleted.

Just then the German chemist, Beckhardt, came up behind both of them and spoke. "I can help, maybe."

Hazzard slapped the small man on the shoulder. "Thank you, Herr Beckhardt. Washington MacGowen, Otto Beckhardt. Herr Beckhardt is a chemist."

Wash shook hands with Beckhardt. "Well, I can certainly use another pair of hands. That's for sure."

Hazzard was satisfied, with Beckhardt's help, Wash would come through for him. "You just get busy with that X-ray and leave the rest to me!" With a light in his eyes that even Wash couldn't interpret, Hazzard strode towards the two controls that held the mighty power of the great volcano in check – the one operating the worm gear in the giant valve, the other which could send a river pouring into the crater. He swung the rheostat needle all the way over.

The impulse from the delicate mechanism inside the glass case was transmitted to the huge electric motor, multiplied a thousand times, till tons of metal revolved as the great valve in the crater cap moved shut.

Then Hazzard opened the other control till a quivering needle on a clock-faced dial registered a flow of water. Tons of it began pouring into the crater. Hazzard was beginning the greatest gamble of his life.

He turned and left the controls for a moment. Something was thudding on the outside of the control-room door.

"Sounds like they got themselves a battering-ram," Jake Cole suggested, as he and Hazzard went to check it out. There was a small sliding panel in the door, a peep-hole covered with a meshed grating. There were indications that the Phoenix had planned to use this room to withstand an assault in case his Indians ever became rebellious.

Hazzard opened the peep-hole and stared out. Sure enough, the Python Men had a log and were going at the door systematically. Hazzard saw a sea of copper faces. Even if Wash and Beckhardt succeeded in condensing the X-ray outfit so they could carry it, it seemed impossible that they would ever get through this cordon of howling savages.

But the Indians were stepping aside now to make way for someone. They were opening a wide path. Through it came a hideous, vulture-like figure. A man with a wizened face and insanely burning eyes. The Phoenix!

Hazzard waited breathlessly. The Phoenix came straight up to the control-room door. He spoke in a quiet voice as though addressing a business confrere. "I see, my friend, that you have succeeded in stirring up quite a bit of trouble in my humble enclave. I believe I have the pleasure of speaking to the famous Captain Hazzard."

"And you would be the Phoenix," confirmed Hazzard grimly. "The madman who thinks he can conquer the entire world."

The Phoenix's eyes darted venomous fire. His thin lips curled back from his yellow teeth. "Fool! Because you have succeeded in barricading yourself in that room with a handful of slaves, you think you are in a position to mock me!" The Phoenix drew himself erect in fierce, bombastic pride and thumped his chest. "You cannot even make terms with me. My faithful Indians will batter the door down presently. Then, every one of your party will be tortured to death...

But because I value the safety of certain instruments I have in there, I'm going to offer you one alternative. Open the door now, come out peacefully, and all of you will be allowed to live."

"As slaves, no doubt," Hazzard finished.

"It is your choice, sir," the Phoenix. "I will not make the offer a second time."

Captain Hazzard laughed. "What you say about the safety of your instruments is well put. And your Indians won't batter this door down. You see, Phoenix, I am going to stop them."

"Oh, and how do you propose to accomplish that feat, my foolhardy friend?"

"Once in the past hour they tasted the wrath of Omoxotl. My red flare and my projected voice drove them out of the python's pit with little trouble. Now, by the wrath of Omoxotl, I'm going to drive them away from this door."

"They are superstitious morons," agreed the Phoenix. "But I am with them now. Nothing you can possibly say to them will have the slightest effect."

"Oh, no?" Captain Hazzard's tone was mocking. "Why don't we let them be the judge of that?" He suddenly spoke a few clipped sentences in the Indian dialect. "Go! Leave this place. Let us come out in peace, or the wrath of the great Omoxotl will descend upon you. I am a white god, a greater god than your master, the Phoenix!"

The jeering voices of the Indians rose. They drove their battering ram against the door more fiercely as the Phoenix spurred them on.

Hazzard spoke in English again, addressing the Phoenix. "I've closed the valve in the crater. I've let loose the underground river!"

"What!" A note of shocked amazement was in the Phoenix's voice. He came nearer the door with his lips sliding away from his teeth again.

Hazzard said, "Listen."

There was a rumbling at his feet. A rumbling that came from the vast depths of the earth, a rumbling that seemed to make the entire mountain quiver.

"The voice of Omoxotl!" cried Hazzard to the Indians.

A sickly, terrible pallor spread over the wizened face of the

Phoenix. He commenced to tremble violently. "Shut it off, you fool!" he screamed, spittle spewing from his cracked, gray lips. "Shut it off...or you'll blow us all to kingdom come!"

Without waiting for Hazzard to reply, he spoke to his Indians. They renewed their attack on the heavy metal door.

Hazzard shouted again in their tongue, "Stop! Stop! The wrath of Omoxotl will be on your heads! The voice of Omoxotl speaks already!"

Finally, some of the Phoenix's Python Men left their places at the log, mumbling fearfully amongst themselves. As they moved away, the Phoenix drew a revolver from his robes and waved it at them.

"Back! I command you! Back!" he shouted in their dialect.

When the hesitant Indians did not move, he deliberately opened fire on them. Hatefully, ruthlessly, he sent bullets into their bodies.

Hearing the shots, Jake looked up at Hazzard. "What's going on out there, boss?"

"He's shooting his own men!" Hazzard said, not believing his own eyes. "He truly is insane."

The Phoenix was a madman now. His eyes rolled. There was a froth on his on his thin, sickly lips and his yellow teeth were like the fangs of a jackal. Fear of him bit into the Indians' hearts, fear momentarily greater than the rumblings beneath their feet. Sullenly, those who had not been shot returned to their places on the battering ram and once more renewed their attack on the door.

The entire chamber was shaking now, but not because of those blows. It was shaking because the whole mountain was quaking, because all of hell was bubbling, seething down there, thousands of feet below the rock. It was shaking because a river of water continued to flow into the super-heated crater and there was no way for the pent-up gases to get out.

Hazzard leaped back to the control boards. Dial needles were quivering, trembling like wild things. A red liquid was pulsing furiously in an upright tube with coils beneath it. He turned the rheostat controlling the giant worm gear a little, opening the great valve a few feet.

A roaring shriek of gas escaping under terrific pressure came from somewhere in the mountain. It was sound that none of them, natives and foreigners alike, would forget as long as they lived. All the furies of hades seemed to be screaming at once. The floor swayed back and forth. The walls started to rattle.

Outside the door, Hazzard heard the frenzied, terrified shouts of the Indians. Their shouts were punctuated by the staccato reports of the Phoenix's gun as he murdered them brutally, drove the rest back to the battering ram even as the ceiling began to come down on their heads.

Hazzard looked across the room and saw Wash and Beckhardt working over the X-ray outfit. Bent, absorbed, Wash's face was as owlish and placid as though he were working over some interesting problem in their Long Island laboratories. He looked at Jake in time to see the big cowboy slide a stick of chewing gum into his mouth lazily as he twirled Hazzard's automatic in his other hand. He'd relieved Mary Parker of it upon their return to the room. His tanned, homely face was the same deadpan as usual. Hazzard knew the wrangler was having the time of his life, caught in the middle of a new adventure.

As for Martin Tracey, he was all over the place, administering to the weak and dehydrated men they had rescued.

Mary Parker was at his side, assuming the role of willing and helpful nurse. Even through the scratches and smears of dirt, her lovely face gave each man she touched a true glimmer of hope.

Hazzard again marveled at her stamina and grit. But she was also a different person now that she had her father with her. It was obvious in her words and movements. There were tears in her eyes, but they were tears of joy. The thought of death didn't seem to trouble her as long as her dad could go out with her.

Hazzard felt a lump in his throat. The lives of all these brave souls depended on him. He was taking long chances. He was gambling with death to keep death at bay. He dare not lose that contest.

He looked out the peep-hole. Most of the Python Men had fled except for the group that the terror of the Phoenix had held together. They were small in number. The corpses of the men he had shot lay slumped on the floor. Hazzard wondered at the awful fear the fiend inspired.

Then Wash spoke above the banshee shriek of the crumbling mountain. "It's ready, Captain! This is about as light as I can make the thing."

He and Beckhardt hefted the X-ray cabinet, which they had stripped of all non-essential parts. In twenty minutes of patient work, Wash had put the experiences of a lifetime into these alterations. They had shifted delicate tubes, changed wiring, disconnected and reconnected batteries.

"It is a vonder..is it not?" Beckhardt said, his pride at the result of their efforts obvious. "A portable X-ray unit. Who would have believed it?"

Hazzard took the instrument from them. He guessed its weighed at about sixty pounds. It was something he could carry easily.

"Well done, gentlemen," he smiled. "Now if you'll just hold it a few more minutes." They took it from him gladly.

He did a strange, desperate thing then...the climax of his hairbreadth plan of escape. He walked to the control boards, shut the great valve again, and deliberately smashed the mechanism with a wrench, wedging it so that the valve couldn't be opened. Then he did the same to the control which governed the flow of water.

He whirled and said to all assembled, "Alright! Let's get out of here!"

CHAPTER FIFTEEN

Death's Gambit

Captain Hazzard retrieved the tiny bomb he'd given Otto Beckhardt earlier and took another one from his belt. He made the whole group retire to the far side of the lab, away from the big door.

He raced forward, placed a bomb close to the door, touched the striker. Then he joined the others against the far wall. "Turn your heads away from the blast and keep your eyes closed till its over!"

A ripping explosion came with a roar that momentarily rose above the rumbling of the mountain. The door was torn from its hinges and crashed outward, killing two Python Men, wounding several others.

It almost struck the Phoenix, but the wily vulture man eluded harm and fled. His savage guard followed after him. At a signal from Captain Hazzard, the people for whose lives he was responsible followed him through the ruined door.

Gun flame lanced down the corridor at them. Bullets whined by their heads. The Phoenix was shooting wildly, furiously. Hazzard moved aside and let Jake Cole, still wielding his Colt .45, come forward and return fire. He kept blasting away until the Phoenix wisely retreated to find cover.

Then they ran along the passage toward a far-off glow that was the light of day. Hazzard and the cowboy had the lead, followed by Wash and Beckhardt still hefting the shrunken X-ray box between them. Next came Martin Tracey with Mary Parker, her father and the other freed slaves.

Hazzard was alert for more trouble. The Phoenix would not simply let them walk out, despite the fact the mountain was starting to collapse all around them. It was as if they were moving though a rolling funhouse in an amusement park. Hazzard knew their enemies would gather somewhere and make a stand.

He saw them grouped together at the mouth of the exit. Spears came his way. Shrieking, angry savages ran to head off the escape of these men who had a short time ago been their abject slaves.

Hazzard touched the striker of another of his mini grenades and hurled it. It was life against life now. The mountain was trembling violently all around them. They must leave it soon or be swept away into oblivion.

The bomb struck the foremost Indians, and they seemed to disintegrate. They died instantly, and the others fell back shrieking. This seemed to be more evidence of the might and wrath of Omoxotl.

They retreated, leaving the passage clear, and they didn't try to molest Hazzard and his party further. But there was another barrier that Hazzard feared far more. Python Men he could fight, with guns, with bombs, with his bare hands even. But that other barrier – dim, intangible, awful – would be flung across the trail, barring their way.

Earthquakes were shaking the sides of the walls. As they passed down the trail, great rocks fell near them. Two men taking up the rear were crushed by a massive boulder before they utter a cry. Hazzard yelled to keep them moving, while he and his men kept a constant look-out to be ready to dodge any new rockfalls. Staring up ahead, Hazzard saw a cliff break away and tumble with a roar like a hundred Niagras. The earth under them was heaving up and down, making it hard to maintain their balance as they hurried along. There was terror in the air – terror, horror, madness. The malignant shadow of the Phoenix seemed to hover over them still.

They came to a bend in the trail, and Hazzard saw the thing he dreaded. The curtain of weird luminescence hung between the two walls of the gorge. It danced, quivered, touched and receded. Even the earthquake tremors which shook the mountain didn't affect it. It seemed worse now, more sinister, more symbolic of the evil of the Phoenix.

Mary Parker clutched her father. Minute by minute, he was slowly regaining some semblance of his old self. Still, some of the slaves, miners and natives, whose nerves had been shattered by their long imprisonment underground, gasped in fear and crowded together. But they saw Captain Hazzard walk steadily on and they followed.

He was close to the Death Curtain now. Then, looking through it, he saw a line of green-plumed Python Men drawn up. The Indians set up savage exultant cries as they saw Hazzard's party. The Tzutuhiles were convinced the Phoenix's death-curtain would destroy escapees.

Captain Hazzard went to Wash and Beckhardt and switched on the X-ray cabinet before taking it from them. He made all the others stand back while he advanced, holding the Roentgen-ray tube before him, letting its rays strike out toward the light curtain.

He walked closer and closer and nothing happened. The waving, shimmering mantle of dread light still hung there. The Indians' cries increased. Hazzard went closer, closer, till his head began to ring, till that strange dizziness came which was the first symptom of a bloodstream being affected. He went closer still, till he could hardly stand. He pushed the power switch of the X-ray machine farther over.

Wash called a warning to him. Hazzard was reeling now, swaying on his feet. Anger, disappointment, despair beat in his brain. They were hemmed in by death. Death behind them in the form of the mighty volcano about to explode. Death in front in that ghastly curtain that seemed to have baffled him.

"Look out, Captain! Don't go any closer! Here, let me hold it."

Wash came forward. Jake and Martin followed. If Captain Hazzard was going to walk into that curtain of death, these loyal friends and assistants wanted to follow him. A lump rose in Hazzard's throat. A haze swam before his eyes. Yes, if he gave the order, they would follow him. They would stay at his side, marching like soldiers in the face of withering fire, marching straight into that lethal light curtain.

Wash was stumbling. Jake's jaws had stopped working and sweat beaded his brow under his stetson. Tracey was pushing forward like a man walking against a hurricane sweeping over a desert. The light was making him dizzy. But they had faith...faith in Captain Hazzard. He had contrived this machine to battle the light waves. He had said it would work. If he said so, it must be so.

Then suddenly the miracle happened. Hazzard trembled, stared. The X-ray cabinet almost slipped from his hands. Then he held it tighter. Ahead of him, straight ahead, where the alpha rays from the mechanism he was holding bisected those other rays, the curtain of death was thinning. The oppressive aura didn't quite touch now. When the shimmering points of light approached there was a weakness, an indecision about them.

Hazzard moved further into them, resolutely, exultantly. Jake, Wash and Tracey followed. Into the Curtain of Death, like four comrades of a lost legion marching their way through terror.

And now the light was melting rapidly, cleaving away, leaving a tunnel for them to pass through. Hazzard called to the others. "Get the girl, Martin. Get her father and have them all come fast. Hurry! There's no telling how long the break will stay open!"

Tracey ran back, rounded up Mary Parker and her father, stirred the dazed men into motion again. Gasping, trembling, they stumbled into the curtain, in through the tunnel that Captain Hazzard had made. On they went, on to where the Tzutuhiles stood waiting for them.

Then another miracle happened, a miracle that followed logically on the heels of this first. Hazzard was ahead, walking bravely toward them, the X-ray cabinet still in his hands. And suddenly, one of the Python Men went down on his knees. He bent his green-plumed head to the dust. He said, "Zuma! Zuma! Master! Master!"

The other Indians did the same. They had seen with their own eyes what the Phoenix had told them could never happen. They had seen men, living men, walk through that curtain of spectral light and survive. They knew now that this tall white man was a god greater than the shriveled, vulture-like being who had ruled them for so long.

A pistol shot rang out and a slug whizzed past Hazzard's head. All eyes turned to look back along the trail. To everyone's astonishment, a lone vulture-like figure appeared running from the mountain, a pistol in his hand. The Phoenix was not about to let his foes get away, even if it meant hunting them down single-handedly.

"You won't escape the wrath of the Phoenix," he cried out, firing several more shots. Those in Hazzard's group and the bewildered Python Men all dove to the ground in hopes of eluding his wild shots.

Without slowing his pace for a second, the crazed would-be conqueror of the world entered the Death Curtain tunnel still firing away. One of his bullets hit the X-ray cabinet in Captain Hazzard's hands and it made a crackling noise and went dead. At that same exact instant, the artificial opening it had manipulated in the light curtain vanished, trapping the Phoenix in the murderous rays. His body came to a stop, as if millions of electrical fingers had taken a hold of him. Pain flooded through every pore of his emaciated body and he began to convulse, a silent scream dying in his ravaged lungs. In an instant, he was enveloped in flames until his entire body became a fiery torch.

Mary Parker gasped and turned her head away as the burning man fell forward a few more feet and then toppled over. His body landed outside the shimmering field, smouldering on the moss covered jungle path. A sour stench rose up from the charred, unmoving corpse.

Hazzard looked from his fallen foe to the destroyed machine in his hands. He silently mused at the ironic twist of fate that had brought about the Phoenix's end. His own bullet had eliminated the safety tunnel, thereby making him the last victim of his own devilish machine, the Death Curtain. It was a fitting end to a monster.

Now the Tzutuhiles fell back peacefully and let Hazzard and his friends pass. And Hazzard spoke a warning to them, "Run! Run for your lives! Huetenzo! I have set my curse on Omoxotl!"

The Indians shot terrified glances at the volcano and the remains of their old master. Then they turned and fled toward the safety of the jungle. Hazzard's party went after them. The ground shaking, a steady roar of rocks sounded all around them as powerful tremors shook down the boulders. Another piece of cliff broke away and almost blocked the trail ahead. They climbed over it and pushed on.

They reached at last the downward slant of the trail before it entered the green wall of the jungle. A sound that was greater than any explosion broke out behind them. A sound that was the living, furious symbol of all tumult lifted its gigantic voice above the mountain. The earth danced. The sky grew dark. Flames shot up from the top of the crater, flames and gas, bearing aloft with tons of structural steel and concrete, tons of riveted steel plate. So much for man's engineering construction.

The Phoenix's lost city was being demolished in grand style.

The mountain had spat the great valve as a monster might spit some unsavory morsel from its throat. But even with the valve gone, the mountain wasn't done with its violence. Those tons of water had built up a pressure in the bowels of the earth that spelled a cataclysm. Lava, hot and livid, was pushing up to the top of the crater with millions of pounds of pressure behind it.

Hazzard led his party into the jungle at a fast clip. The further away from the doomed Omoxotl, the better. They had entered the interior just as the first small stones the volcano had disgorged and commenced hurtling down. They made their way through a green world of roaring sounds and somber shadows. Monkeys fled through the high canopy chattering in panic. Parrots screeched past them as they ran. Jaguars slunk ahead of them along the trail, for once forgetting their terror and hatred of human beings in the greater fear of the erupting volcano. Omoxotl was on the rampage. Terror's Shadow was living up to its name.

They were five miles away when the biggest explosion of all came, a booming upheaval that blew off the whole top of Omoxotl!

The resulting concussion sent them all falling to soft ground.

After it had subsided, when the fires began flickering out and a slow, somber brooding peace returned to the jungle, Mary Parker spoke with a tinge of regret, "Now we will never know who the

"Flames shot up from the top of the crater, flames and gas, bearing aloft with tons of structural steel and concrete, tons of riveted steel plate."

Phoenix was."

"Oh, but I think somebody her can answer that question, Miss Parker." Hazzard came over to the fallen tree on which the girl and her father, Franklin Parker were resting. The engineer was looking at Hazzard with a light of recognition in his eyes. With effort, he opened his mouth to speak for the first time.

"The Phoenix," the raspy voice said, "was my partner, Kurt Gordon."

Mary Parker couldn't believe her father's revelation.

"I found evidence suggesting it," Captain Hazzard added, giving the older gentlemen time to catch his breath. "When I went through the papers in the safe. Then later, when I beheld him at the lab door, I realized he, like the men he had enslaved, was also a victim of the sulfuric gases. Am I right, Mister Parker?"

"Yes, yes. Those gases changed him, shriveled his body; made him look so horrible that even his own family wouldn't recognize him. I suspect it's also what drove the poor devil mad."

Mary Parker was still having trouble believing the villain had been someone she had once called a friend. "But how did it happen, Father?"

"Remember, Mary, Gordon had come down here years ago, before the rest of us."

"Exactly," Hazzard took up the narrative. "He must have been studying Omoxotl, dreaming secret dreams of power. He probably used money that belonged to your father's partnership with him to lay the foundation of his project. But he had to have more money than that. He got it cleverly. It necessitated a connection with a New York gang, however."

"Why is that?" the girl asked, wanting to hear the entire story now. The rest of them gathered around as well.

"Jewels," said Captain Hazzard. "Right, Wash. You and the others worked there. Explain what Gordon was doing for us."

"Gladly," the bald-headed former academician beamed, delighted to take center stage. Gordon…or the Phoenix…used the heat of the volcano to make synthetic gems that couldn't be told from nature's originals – sapphires, emeralds and diamonds. The man was creating an empire of wealth beyond imagining. That's why these Indians were so free with their emeralds."

Hazzard came over to Wash and picked up the tale. "That's also the major reason they were so loyal to him. And his New York gang was his outlet. The jewels were smuggled into the U.S., sold at a big profit, and the millions that Gordon got for them financed his mad ambitions for world dominion."

"Hot doggie," Jake whistled, around a wad of chewing gum. "Wait till old Bill Crawley gets a wind of this story, Captain. He's going to bust a stitch writing this one up."

Hazzard gave his friend a quiet smile. The adventure was over. All that remained now was for them to make it back to the friendly village of the Chicastenagos and from there get word to Tyler Randall via a government runner.

The crater of Omoxotl, the lost city, was still smoking. It was a giant sinister torch lifting up into the dome of the sky. It was the funeral pyre of the Phoenix.

EPILOGUE

Print the Romance

T wo weeks later, true to Jake Cole's prediction, ace reporter William Crawly sat in Captain Hazzard's office jotting down notes feverishly with his short, worn pencil. Washington MacGowen had come in, coffee cup in hand, just as Hazzard was ending his report.

"Holy smoke," Crawley exclaimed, folding up his notebook and putting it away in his coat pocket along with his stubby pencil. "What a yarn. Geez, Captain. My pulp friend, Chester Hawks, will eat this stuff up with a spoon. Lost jungle cities, a lovely skirt in trouble and a bizarre, evil villain. It will practically sell itself."

Sitting at his ornate, teak wood desk, Captain Hazzard steepled his fingers together and reminded the reporter of their arrangement. "As long as every penny of profit goes to charity, I've no problems with this Hawks fellow detailing our exploits in his magazine."

"But of course," Crawley affirmed, snatching his fedora off the table as he rose to depart. He saw MacGowen for the first time and nodded.

"So, do you have a title for this latest piece of purple prose," the scientist asked amusingly.

"You bet," Crawley said, waving his two hands in front of his face and imagining the banner over a page. "We'll call it *Python Men of the Lost City*! Doesn't it just ring?"

Wash arched an eyebrow indicating concern. "You may have a slight problem with that particular title, Bill."

"Oh? How so?"

"Well, you see, there are no pythons in Guatemala. Or anywhere else in South America, for that matter."

Crawley tilted his hat back and scratched his temple, looking back

142

at Hazzard, who had a silly grin on his handsome face. "Hey, is he telling it straight, Captain?"

"I'm afraid so, Crawley. I never once said the word python in my story. What we encountered were anacondas, and that is what I told you."

Crawley looked from Hazzard to MacGowen and then shrugged. "Aw, come on, guys, you got to give us a break here. Nobody out there is going to buy a book called *Anaconda Men of the Lost City*. In the paper biz, when romance butts head with the facts, you gotta print the romance.

"Adios, amigos." And with that the savvy newshound made his exit.

Wash and Captain Hazzard started laughing.

The End

Captain Hazzard as rendered by Jay Piscopo

BACK IN PRINT

Three years ago, I made a dream come true by sitting down and rewriting, start to finish, a special pulp novel: *Captain Hazzard: The Python Men of the Lost City.* I'd read Bob Weinberg's facsimile edition twenty years earlier, and since that time I'd harbored a dream of someday sitting down to write brand new Captain Hazzard adventures. Sometimes God is truly kind, and circumstances occurred in such a way to make that dream a reality.

James Chambers, my good friend and colleague, had introduced me to editor/publisher Vincent Sneed of Die Monster Die Press. Sneed was putting together an anthology of stories about strong, heroic women and invited me to participate. I gave him a story called "Fury in Vermont," and he accepted it for publication. Writing that story gave me a desire to write other pulp stories, and I asked Sneed if he would be interested in looking at them. He in turn suggested I seek out Ron Hanna who, via his Wild Cat Books, published pulp reprints. I contacted Hanna and explained to him that what I wanted to do was publish new fiction starring classic pulp heroes. Outside of a few amateurish fanzines, no one was doing this at the time.

Hanna liked the idea, and we got the ball rolling. The first classic pulp characters we reintroduced were in the crossover story I'd written with Gordon Linzner, *The Hounds of Hell.* In this adventure, the Moon Man, who originally appeared in *10 Detective Aces,* crosses paths with Doctor Satan, the villain from *Weird Tales.* It was the first time two pulp characters had ever met in this fashion, and the confrontation between hero and villain fueled the plot of the entire book. *The Hounds of Hell* did well enough for us to continue our partnership. Thus was Airship 27 Productions born.

When Hanna asked what I wanted to do next, I remembered Captain Hazzard and told him of my desire to do new adventures of this one-shot wonder. By now, my friend and fellow writer, Martin Powell, had agreed to co-write this brand new Champion of Justice tale. No sooner had we started writing the actual book when Powell found himself bogged down with other commitments, and it appeared that our book would be put on hold for a while. Which was when I remembered that long ago dream of rewriting *Python Men of the Lost City.*

While waiting for Powell to return, I sat down with my battered, dog-eared copy of that old facsimile digest and began in earnest to fix this sixty-eight-year-old pulp thriller.

I invented two characters, filled in the plot holes and added entire new chapters to straighten the narrative. It took me just under two months to do the job. When finished, I was satisfied that it was a better book, but the final verdict would lie with pulp fans. Hanna took the book, got it published and distributed. The year was 2007. Both of us traveled to Pulp Con that year and debuted this new version to attending fans. Much to my delight, the book was extremely well received, and some fans made a point of seeking out reprints of the original work to compare with our new version.

They were excited about my plans for further Captain Hazzard adventures, which inspired me to get moving on those as well. By now, Powell had wrapped up his other business, and within six months of releasing *Captain Hazzard: Python Men of the Lost City,* we then published the first new Hazzard adventure since his solo appearance in 1938 with *Captain Hazzard: Citadel of Fear.* The following year, I once again rewrote an early Paul Chadwick novel as *Captain Hazzard: Curse of the Red Maggot.* Finally, last year saw the publication of our fourth in this continuing series, *Captain Hazzard: Cavemen of New York.*

Of course, life is a constantly changing process, and shortly after the printing of that second Captain Hazzard book, we parted company with Wild Cat Books. They continued to sell our titles and then eventually made the decision to remove them from their catalog. We took charge and made decision to reprint them via our new publishing partner, Cornerstone Book Publishers. Which is why you are now holding the second edition of Airship 27 Productions' Captain Hazzard: Python Men of the Lost City. You have my word that this edition will not be going out of print anytime soon.

All that remains now is for us to reprint *Captain Hazzard: Citadel of Fear,* and all our Hazzard titles will be once again be available. It's our sincerest hope to reach that goal by the end of this year. Once that happens, I will be turning all my focus on writing new Hazzard books. In the meantime, Airship 27 is flying high these days with over a dozen great pulp titles in our catalog, all of which can be found at our on-line store, http://stores.lulu.com/airship27. Books sold there are always 25-percent off retail prices as our way of saying thanks to all of you for supporting our efforts.

Coming up in the months ahead, look for *Dan Fowler G-Man, The Green Lama* and a book we're really excited about, *Sherlock Holmes, Consulting Detective.* So stay tuned and as always, thanks.

Ron Fortier
22 May 2009
(www.Airship27.com)
(Airship27@comcast.net)

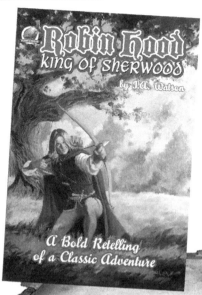
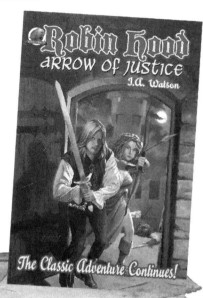

Situated in the rural back country of Edwardian England is an old, mysterious house whose unique owner earns his living as a Spirit-Breaker, a hunter of ghosts. A former military veteran, Sgt. Roman Janus has devoted his life to aid those haunted, both emotionally and physically by obsessive wraiths whose spirits are still anchored to our world.

Airship 27 Productions is thrilled to present *Sgt.Janus – Spirit Breaker* by Jim Beard. Part detective, part occultist, Janus is himself a man of mystery whose own past is shrouded and the motivations behind his calling kept hidden. Within this volume you will find eight tales as narrated by his clients, each with his or her own perspective on this uncanny hero and his amazing career. Filled with suspense, terror and agonizing pathos, each a solid mesmerizing journey into the unknown world beyond.